RUINED HEARTS

SUMMER COOPER

MIRANDA STANLEY

Lovy Books Ltd
20-22 Wenlock Road
London N1 7GU

Created with Vellum
Cover by SC Creative

ALSO BY

Also by Miranda Stanley

Heart Shaped Chaos
Be Mine Tonight
A Forbidden Guardian (FREE ebook)
Escape to His Arms
You Can't Be Mine
I Still Hate You
Yours Always
Take Me Home
Tricked and Treated
Candy Cane Kisses
He's Such A D*ck
His Tokens

Also by Summer Cooper

DARK DESIRES
A billionaire dark romance series
Dark Desire (FREE ebook!)

Dark Rules
Dark Secret
Dark Time
Dark Truth

BARRE TO BAR

A billionaire second chance series
Dancing With Lies (FREE ebook!)
Dancing With Temptation
Dancing With Doubt
Dancing With Guilt
Dancing With Redemption

TWISTED INTENTION

A billionaire revenge romance series
Twisted Beauty (FREE ebook!)
Twisted Love
Twisted Fate

Mafia's Obsession

A hot mafia romance series
Mafia's Dirty Secret (FREE ebook!)
Mafia's Fake Bride
Mafia's Final Play

Screaming Demons

An MC romance series full of suspense
Rough Start (FREE ebook!)
Rough Ride
Rough Choice
Rough Return
Rough Patch
Rough Road

Rough Trip
Rough Night
Rough Love

Check out Summer's entire collection at
www.summercooper.com/books

1

Robin

New Orleans, 1977

I inspected the tiny hotel room I would be calling home for the next month, at the very least, and felt my whole body deflate with disappointment. But what did I really expect for the money I'd paid? It was the cheapest motel I could find in New Orleans with access to the shops and bars within walking distance. I'd told the motel manager I was here to write a story, but I was really running from my life. A life I definitely did not want to think about at the moment.

Dropping my bag on the bed, I tried not to think about how many feet had walked across the dark brown shag carpet since this pink monstrosity of a motel had been built in the 1950's, 20 plus years ago, or how many heads had hit the undoubtedly yellow pillows. I ignored the stale, lingering scent of pets and tobacco and went out to my car. I grabbed the travel trunk out of the back of my car and went back into the hotel.

Once I had the ugly yellow and brown comforter and sheets stripped, with my own pure white bedding in its place, I sprawled out on the bed that smelled like home now and sighed. What else was I supposed to do? I'd been up since 5 am and the sun was just going down on what promised to be a rather humid night. I looked at the slot machine on the side of the bed that controlled the vibrating mechanism of the bed and grimaced.

I didn't want to know how many quarters had gone into that machine. But a bit of a buzz might do me some good. The mirror in the little alcove where the sinks stood showed me, I needed to brush my hair and maybe change my shirt. My bell bottom jeans were fine, if a little faded. I kicked off the running shoes I'd had on all day, put on a pair of soft loafers, and changed into an indigo blue shirt. The pointed lapels seemed to be arrows shooting at my nipples, and I wondered if that was the subliminal point.

A quick brush through the long, black hair on my head tamed it into a straight waterfall of dark silk. I wasn't one for makeup so my tanned skin looked healthy, clean, acceptable to me. As I stared at myself in the mirror my thoughts tried to turn to the woman whose face mirrored my own, a woman dead and buried now.

"No, that's enough of that," I said to the woman in the mirror and blinked in surprise. Why had I said that out loud? I grimaced at myself, hiding my brown eyes for a moment before I turned to leave the motel. Grabbing my bag and the keys, I locked the door and headed down the street, looking for a bar close to the motel so I wouldn't have to stumble home in the dark.

Through the palm trees and hedges, I saw a neon sign

towards the back of the motel. Technically, the building was on the street behind the motel, but it was practically in my back yard. That was close enough for me. My stomach rumbled, reminding me I'd skipped lunch, so I headed for the diner to the right of the motel office first, looking for something quick to fill the hole in my stomach.

The dour redheaded waitress recommended the po' boy sandwich so I found out what exactly that was 10 minutes later. Stuffed between sliced French bread I found a pile of tomatoes, lettuce, and remoulade sauce smothering a larger pile of fried shrimp. I enjoyed every bite of it, despite my initial worry that it would be too heavy for me.

Once outside, I inhaled deeply, ignoring the overwhelming scent of exhaust and found that, beneath the modern smells of cars and restaurants, there was a deep earthy scent that called to me. It smelled entirely different from New York, closer to Mother Nature, despite the modern trappings of city life. I wasn't here to enjoy the scenery, however. I was here to find a killer.

I headed in the direction of the bar, ready to escape the memories, if only for a little while.

"Double shot of Jameson, please," I said to the woman behind the bar. "Ice in a separate glass as well, please."

What can I say? I'm polite.

"Here you are, sweetie," the dark-haired woman with pretty brown eyes and full lips said.

For a moment, I considered whether she would do for the night, but decided against it. I was new to New Orleans and knew it wasn't New York. I'd just get myself in trouble with even a slight attempt at flirtation with her.

I'm not choosy when it comes to gender. In New York City, I could have my choice of bed companions, but here? Not yet, not until I knew a little more about the place.

"You're not from around here," the pretty woman said, her eyes twinkling at me, making me wonder if I was wrong, after all. But then, she was a bartender, it was her job to keep the drinks flowing, by whatever means necessary, right? "Where ya from?"

I liked her voice, but the question put me on edge. It wasn't that I didn't want to talk about where I was from, it was that I didn't really want to get to know a stranger that would want to know my past. That was something I didn't want to talk about, at all.

"New York City, but I'm moving down here for work," I said, lying only a little. I wasn't sure if I was staying here or not.

"Ah, I'd love to live in New York, but New Orleans is pretty special, too," she said in that slightly husky voice of hers before her eyes spotted a man at the end of the bar. She went down to replace the empty beer bottle he waved at her with a full one.

I poured most of my drink into the glass of ice, with a slice of lemon, but left a small measure to sip at while the ice melted into the rest. I looked around and spotted a pool table through a doorway. Not interested in that at all.

The place had started to fill up by the time my ice melted enough to cut the whiskey in the glass. I watched the waitress for entertainment, enjoying the view as she smiled at patrons, filled their drink orders, then moved to the next one along.

"You want another, honey?" she asked once she'd made her way back to me.

"Yes, please," I hadn't made up my mind until she asked, but yeah, I'd stay here a little while longer. Maybe somebody more interesting would show up. If not, I'd go back to the motel and try again tomorrow.

"What's your name?"

I looked at her, wondering if I should give her my real name or be someone else to her. After a moment of mental gymnastics over should I, shouldn't I, I decided to tell her the truth.

"I'm Robin Rodriguez." I answered with a soft smile, hoping I hadn't made a mistake.

"Hi Robin, I'm Belinda Murphy. Nice to meet you," the woman replied, holding out her hand, her pretty slim fingers tipped with red-painted fingernails. I liked her hands.

I shook her hand politely, letting her warm touch go with a breath of regret. We both looked away from each other when the bell over the door dinged. A tall man walked in, aviator sunglasses perched on top of his blond head.

Obviously, he was a busy if he still had his sunglasses on at 7:30 in the evening. I heard a sound from Belinda and glanced at her, peeling my eyes away from the handsome man that needed a shave, his jaw a hard ridge as he looked around before he walked towards me.

Belinda's eyebrows pulled together, her face a frown of anger. She must know the guy and whatever it was she knew made her dislike him. That didn't matter to me, maybe they used to date, and he'd broken it off. Before I could decide what the story was there, he sat down on the stool to the left of mine and ordered a scotch.

I watched the pair from the corner of my eye, catching how he looked resigned as she turned away. Belinda's own jaw tightened as she moved around the bar, grabbing a glass, turned the bottle upside down, then handed the glass over to the man.

"Thanks, Belinda," he said softly, his voice a soothing, husky burr.

I pretended to ignore him when he pulled out a packet of cigarettes and offered me one. I wasn't interested in his smokes, it was his body I was interested in. He was lean but muscular, his gray eyes peering out from deep set sockets.

This was a game I'd played before, cool and aloof, to gain their interest, until I decided whether I wanted them.

THE DIMLY LIT bar smelled of smoke and beer as every patron in the place seemed to light up at the same time. Thank goodness the door was open.

The people inside were a mix of different races and backgrounds, but there was something else about them, something that set them apart. I noticed it for the first time as the man took his cigarettes away and lit one. I could feel it in the air now that he was beside me, a sense of power and danger that sent a shiver down my spine. And all of them felt it too.

From the corner of my eye, I watched him as he sipped at his drink and then sighed. He was quiet, handsome, with an air of strength and danger that was impossible to ignore. I didn't notice I'd turned my head to look at him more closely until he raised his glass to me. I blushed, feeling my face flush red.

He smiled without any other movement, his body radiating heat and confidence from his stool beside me.

"My name is Asa. What's yours?" he asked in that deep-timbered voice that washed over me, making my skin tighten. It was a deep voice, smooth, like honey. I felt myself melting, my intention to play my usual game fading away.

"I'm Robin. Nice to meet you," I tilted my nearly empty

glass at him, putting it down. I'd wait for more of the ice to melt before I finished it.

"New in town?" He asked, his tone polite.

"I guess a lot of people wander over from the motel then?" I questioned, assuming he was local. If he wasn't, Belinda wouldn't have reacted that way.

"They do, yes. I haven't seen you before and I've lived here my whole life," he answered with a slight shrug.

I couldn't help but feel drawn to him. There was something about Asa that made me want to know him more, something dark and mysterious that I couldn't quite put my finger on.

I didn't want to seem too eager, so I took a slow sip of my drink, savoring the warm, smoky flavor. Asa took a drag of his cigarette, the cherry glowing bright in the dim light.

"So, what brings you to New Orleans?" he asked, his gray eyes focused on me.

I hesitated for a moment, knowing I didn't want to reveal my true reasons for being there. But there was something in Asa's gaze that made me want to trust him, to open up to him. That was very dangerous for me, and I knew I should end the conversation but couldn't.

"I'm a writer," I said finally, taking another sip of my drink. "I came down here to do some research for my next book."

Asa arched an eyebrow, a small smile playing at the corners of his lips.

"So, what's your book about?" he asked, his voice low and smooth. "Voodoo queens and moss-draped plantation homes?"

My lips quirked up at the corners, amused at his question. I wasn't there to write a book, but he wouldn't find that out from me. I probably wouldn't even see him again after tonight, and that was just fine with me. Exactly what I was after, actually.

"It's a mystery novel set in New Orleans," I answered, feeling a little more at ease now that we had a topic to discuss. "I'm trying to get a feel for the city, its people, its culture. And no, no moss-draped mansions or voodoo queens in sight."

"Something original then, I can dig that," he nodded, a smile curving the left corner of his mouth. "So long as not all of us are painted as either criminals or crazy Cajuns with a blood vendetta. We're a lot more than that, you know?"

"What are you then? Tell me," I asked, holding up my glass to Belinda as she walked by, a panicked look on her face as she approached me. I gave her a questioning look, but she shook her head and took my glass.

Asa ignored our exchange and snuffed out his cigarette. He took another sip of his drink, his gaze coming back up to meet mine. I watched as his tongue came out to wet his lips before he spoke.

"New Orleans is a city full of secrets," he said cryptically. "It can be dangerous to dig too deep."

I felt a chill run down my spine at his words, wondering if he knew something I didn't. But the thrill of danger only made me more curious, more intrigued by this man who seemed to be warning me about the dark underbelly of the city.

"I'll keep that in mind," I said with a brief smile, finishing my drink. "Thanks for the warning."

Asa smiled back, his lips curving up into a mischievous grin. "Anytime. And if you ever need someone to show you around this city, you know who to call."

I laughed, feeling a rush of excitement at his offer. "I just might take you up on that."

Asa finished his drink and stood up from his stool, towering over me. He reached out a hand and I took it, feeling a jolt of electricity as our palms met.

"It was nice meeting you, Robin," he said, his voice low and husky. "I hope to see you again soon."

With that, he turned and walked out of the bar, leaving me feeling both exhilarated and intrigued. As I watched him go, I couldn't help but wonder what secrets he was hiding, and what kind of dangerous world lay beneath the surface of this city. All I knew about the place were things I'd read in books or seen on television. And that a killer lived here.

"Don't get involved with him," Belinda hissed as he walked away, sliding two more glasses my way, one containing whiskey, the other holding ice and a slice of lemon. One more for the road I thought as I turned back to her.

"Why not?" I asked, my gaze back on hers. Her eyes were a darker shade of brown than mine. Mine had an orange tint and flecks of green here and there. Hers were much darker, almost black.

"Because he's trouble, that's why. I wouldn't even let him in here if it weren't for the fact...," she started to answer but stopped, paused, then continued. "If it wasn't for the fact that he's a local, let's say *businessman*, and he brings a lot of business my way."

"I don't know what's happened between you two," I replied, looking at her. "But I'm not interested in long-term anything. Don't worry, I know what I'm doing."

"I hope so, because Asa Kelley is not what you think he is, I guarantee that," Belinda said cryptically then wandered off after that, her patrons at the other end of the bar wanting more drink.

I decided to finish mine and head back to the motel. I'd

be going back alone, but maybe that was for the best. What I needed was rest, but I doubt I'll get any. Sex was a good distraction, guaranteed to get me to sleep when done with the right partner. Tonight, I'd have to wing it.

What did Belinda mean by businessman? Was it a euphemism or was the guy in a legit business? If that air of danger around him was any indication, I doubted anything he did was legit.

2

———

Robin

I stood in the alcove between the bathroom and the bedroom, my nightgown clinging to my body, the sweat running off me in rivulets. A quick glance in the mirror showed red-rimmed eyes and a pale face. I could feel my hair matted and crunchy from the sweat and the tears I had shed. I shuddered at the memory of the fire.

It had felt so real, the heat blistering my skin as I tried to save my mother, Rose, and my sister, Angela, from the burning house. I could still feel the pain in my chest from the smoke I had inhaled, the terror at not being able to reach them no matter how much I wanted to help. I wanted to forget the nightmare, to erase it from my mind.

I stepped into the shower, the cold water cascading down my body, washing away the sweat that coated me. I felt the tension start to ease away, the fear of the nightmare washing away from me as the water heated up. The problem was, I thought as shampoo washed down my body, that nightmare was a memory, a memory I desperately wanted to forget.

The sound of the rushing water did little to drown out the memory of my mother and my sister's screams, but the moment passed, and I could breathe again. I walked out of the shower feeling more like myself, my skin pink from the hot water and the cool air. I put on a pair of black jeans with a black, slouchy t-shirt and grabbed my bag, determined to take my mind off the nightmare that replayed throughout the night until I gave up and got in the shower.

I opened the door of my room and stepped out into the parking lot, the smell of jasmine and dark, murky water heavy in the early morning air. I made my way to the nearby diner, feeling the warmth of the rising sun on my skin.

I ordered a plate of grits, sausage, and eggs from a smiling but tired looking brunette waitress. A sip of coffee cleared away the cobwebs in my brain as the smell of bacon frying in the kitchen made my stomach grumble in anticipation. When my food came, I ate quickly, my appetite for food stronger than it had been in days.

All I'd really wanted for weeks now was alcohol, though it never drowned out the memories. It did help to get me to sleep, though, even if I woke up with a headache and an upset stomach. Today, though, I wanted food, needed it, so I ate everything and then thought about whether I should order something more. I decided to wait until lunchtime. I didn't want to end up being too full. I'd only want to lay back down, and I had things to do today.

With the decision made, I wiped my mouth, paid my bill, and left the diner, my thoughts turning to exploration. I walked to one of the streetcar stops and climbed on board the streetcar that promised to take me along the Rampart/St. Claude streetcar line. This line would take me by the famous St. Louis Cemetery. As the streetcar rattled along the tracks, I looked out the window at the city, taking in the crowds of smiling people, the smells of water, spices, and seafood that filled the air, and the sights of a city wrested from the swamp centuries ago. Here was a city full of life, excitement, and everything I could think of for sale. I was amazed at how vibrant it was. I guess I expected the South, especially this far south, to be too hot to move and teetering on the edge of immobility.

I stepped off the streetcar at North Rampart and began to wander, taking in the sights, learning the layout of the place. Everywhere I looked, there were signs of voodoo, Louisiana pride with the purples, greens and golds of Mardi Gras, and crawfish everything. Already, the place was digging its way into my heart, but I wasn't here to fall in love with the city.

Still, I couldn't help but be curious about all of it, even if I was more interested in learning about the Irish descendants in the city. Everyone seemed to know about the French and Spanish that came to Louisiana, families that built great wealth on the back of African slaves. A lot of people even knew that Louisiana had a large population of Italians, as well, but none of those families interested me. It was the Irish families that came to work on the docks and in the shipyards that interested me.

But it was one family in particular that I wanted to find, that drove me to come to Louisiana and seek out people I should do my best to avoid. The Hawkins family was rarely talked about, rarely pictured in newspapers or talked about on the local news. They avoided the media and had good reason to, when one considered the family was involved in some of the worst illegal activity in the country.

I paused at a cafe, ordering cafe au lait and beignets so I

could sit still for a few minutes as the memories plagued me. Last year, my sister vanished for months and when she came home, she whispered her story to me, as if she was afraid the man that took her would hear her and come back for her.

The night she vanished from my life, Angela went out to a nightclub with someone she met at a bar. He'd been handsome, charming, everything she could dream of, she'd told me. They'd had a great night and she'd had a few drinks. Nothing that would leave her intoxicated or cause her to pass out. They'd agreed to go to an all-night diner, she'd said, and the moment she stepped out of the nightclub was the last thing she remembered. She woke up the next morning, bound and gagged, in his backseat.

She'd tried to signal for help but the tinted windows in the back of the car made it impossible for anyone to see her. He'd stopped eventually at a warehouse close to water. She'd known she was in Louisiana, she just didn't know where. Once inside the warehouse, the man assigned her a cubicle that contained a camp cot and little more. He'd chained her to the floor and given her a bucket as a toilet.

When she tried to ask where she was and why he was doing this, he slapped her so hard so fell to the floor. He gave her another when she begged him to let her go. That's when she heard the other sounds in the warehouse, the moans and cries of other women, the whispers of others, the laughter of one. She wasn't alone in there, but she didn't know how many other women were hidden behind the dividers that made up her cubicle.

She didn't know how long she'd been there before a man came to her, a man that took her out of the warehouse. He'd been so golden and full of light that she thought he was an angel. Angela actually scoffed as she told me how she'd thought he'd come to save her and she'd cried tears of relief, but those tears soon turned to horror when she was taken to his penthouse and chained to the bed in his bedroom.

SHE WOULDN'T TALK about what happened after that, but I could imagine. I didn't want to imagine, but with my brain, always overactive anyway, I imagined the hours, the days, the things she'd endured. Even now, I would find my mind wandering to what Angela must have endured, to the hopelessness she must have felt, and it took my breath away.

I guess that's what really fuels my nightmares, how utterly helpless I felt about the entire situation. The things Angela endured at the hands of that raving maniac were horrific, and would leave physical and mental scars for the rest of her. Though that life was short. The fire made sure of that.

My thoughts wandered back to what she'd revealed to me, to the vacant way she'd stared at the walls as the words poured out of her. Angela hadn't just been held for a few days, then tossed away. Oh no. Her captor wanted to make sure he'd had every last drop of her he'd wanted before he disposed of her. Only, Angela wasn't about to sit around and wait for that day. She'd been brave, determined, desperate to get back home to Mom and I.

For weeks, she'd searched his room for a way to get free, until one day, she'd looked at where the chain was bolted to the floor. It had taken her another two weeks to work the four bolts free. But she was faced with another problem at that point: how to get out of the penthouse.

The door opened onto an elevator, but there was

another door, a door that opened onto a stairwell. She'd only had on a nightgown when she'd made her flight down those stairs, and she'd stepped out of the building with bare feet. Still, she'd raced away from the building until she'd run right into a policeman, clinging to him as she begged for help.

She'd refused to file a report, but the older cop was a kind man, the kind she'd stopped hoping existed. He'd taken her to his sister's place, got her some clothes, and put her on the bus to New York. He'd wanted to call my mother and I, but she couldn't remember our phone numbers.

All those weeks, I'd searched for Angela, not knowing if she was alive or dead. When she showed up at my apartment, her face flooded with tears, I'd taken her into my living room and held her as she sobbed for what felt like hours. I did manage to convince her to go to the hospital but she wouldn't file a police report. The man she knew as Ryan Hawkins knew where Mom and I lived, had rattled off our addresses to Angela, and had threatened to kill us if she even so much as thought about escaping.

That fear had paralyzed her for days, but after a few nights of being unable to escape him, that fear had turned into something else. Terror that she'd never get away from him. Angela was terrified that he'd show up, but Mom and I assured her we'd all be safe.

Staring at the congealed powdered sugar on my dough-nuts, I knew I'd lied to her. I'd had no idea how that man had been willing to do anything to get her back. And when it became clear he wouldn't, that he couldn't snatch her because she never left the house, he'd burned down the house to try and force her out.

I'd been there that night and every night since she came home. I'd fallen asleep on the couch, in front of the TV, when I'd smelled smoke. By then, the fire had crept up the stairs and into their rooms. I hadn't been able to get them out and they'd both died in the flames. I'd only left the house because a firefighter dragged me out of the house. If she hadn't had the shield on her helmet down, I'd have clawed her eyes out to get back inside. She'd held me down as I screamed for my mother and sister, but not without tears filling her own eyes.

Now, I was in the city Angela had been dragged to, hunting down a family I wanted to annihilate. I'd lied to everyone that asked me why I was in Louisiana. I'd told them I was there to do a story. Some assumed it was a news story, others thought I was writing a book. What I was really there for was revenge.

I'd find this Ryan Hawkins and I'd burn down his home. I'd burn down every home of his family, and hopefully, I'd find the warehouse where he kept the women and set them all free. Then burn down that warehouse, too. So yeah, New Orleans was beautiful, so beautiful I could easily fall in love with it, but I wasn't capable of love.

My heart had shriveled up and died the night Ryan Hawkins took my family from me. Vengeance *would* be mine. I just had to lay low, stay out of sight of anyone that might tip him off, and wait for my chance. It would come. I just had to be patient.

I'd already paid for my untouched coffee and dough-nuts, so I got up and left the cafe, headed back towards the motel. I wasn't sure how to find this guy, but I figured a search of the phonebook would be a good place to start.

While I walked down the streets, I scanned every face, looking for any sign of recognition. My sister was two years younger than me, but we'd been spitting images of each other, to the point people had often assumed we were twins.

If Ryan saw me, or one of his people, they might assume I was Angela, and I couldn't let that happen. I kept my head down, hiding behind a pair of sunglasses and a hat. I didn't want to draw any attention to myself, not yet.

I found myself walking towards the French Quarter, the vibrant sounds of jazz filling the air. People were everywhere, laughing and drinking, enjoying the day, even at this early hour. It was a stark contrast to the darkness that had consumed my life.

I'd never been one for crowds, but something about the energy of the city pulled me closer. I walked down Bourbon Street, trying my best to blend in with the tourists and revelers. I was tempted to stop in one of the bars, to have a bartender pour me a tall, cool drink of anything, but I'd wait until this evening, until I was close enough to the motel I could get back to without too many problems, even on my own.

I continued walking, enjoying the warm sun on my skin. When I found the stop for the streetcars, I hopped aboard and made my way back to my room. I'd already done mountains of research, trying to find information about Ryan Hawkins, but had turned up nothing. I'd keep at it, though, hoping something would turn up that could help me.

I considered calling that cop, that detective, the man that saved my sister and sent her back to me, even if it was only for a little while, but I didn't want to involve him. I had criminal activities planned that he might put a stop to if he found out about them. Plus, I didn't want him to get into any kind of trouble for helping me. My sights were set on Ryan Hawkins and nobody else.

3

Robin

The bar near my temporary home seemed to have a life of its own, pulsating with energy like the beating heart of the city. The dim lighting cast shadows that danced along the walls, like memories come to life. Laughter bubbled through the air, a rich mixture of bass and soprano tones that filled every gap in the room, while the smooth sounds of jazz music drifted from the corner where a small band played with fervor.

Behind the worn wooden bar, Belinda moved with a fluid grace that seemed almost otherworldly. Her shiny black hair, which hung loose down her back, seemed to catch even the faintest glimmers of light. Her delicate features were animated as she served drinks to the patrons, her warm smile never faltering as she effortlessly juggled conversations and orders. Though she was petite, there was an undeniable strength in the way she carried herself, a fierce loyalty evident in the way she kept a protective eye on her regulars.

"Evenin', Robin," Belinda greeted me as I approached the bar, her brown eyes sparkling with genuine affection. "What'll it be tonight?"

"Same as last time, please," I replied, my voice barely audible over the din of voices and music.

"Comin' right up." She flashed another one of her captivating smiles before turning to pour my drink. As I waited, I couldn't help but marvel at how effortlessly she navigated the chaos around her, a beacon of warmth and comfort in this wild, unpredictable world.

When she handed me my glass, with an extra glass of ice and a slice of lemon beside it, I raised it to her in silent appreciation before taking a slow sip, letting the fiery liquid burn a path down my throat. The smoky taste lingered on my tongue, a welcome distraction from the thoughts that threatened to consume me.

"Thanks, Belinda," I murmured, my eyes scanning the crowded bar for any sign of the man who had been haunting my dreams.

"Anytime, darlin'," she replied, her voice carrying a hint of concern as she studied my face. "Just remember, I'm here if you need me."

I nodded, grateful for her offer of friendship as I tried not to make it obvious I was watching for Asa Kelley, the reason I found myself in this bar. It was only a matter of time before our paths crossed again, and I could feel my heart racing with anticipation as I imagined what would happen between us.

The man was trouble. Belinda had already warned me about that, but I didn't want him as a life partner or even as a friend. I just wanted sex from him, nothing more. If I exhausted myself with him, with his body, I might be able to sleep tonight without the nightmares waking me up.

The patrons of the bar were an eclectic mix, reflecting the true essence of New Orleans. From the young tourists seeking a taste of excitement to the seasoned locals who carried the weight of their stories on their shoulders, each person seemed to be searching for something, whether it was solace, companionship, or simply a reprieve from the burdens of life.

Their conversations melded together into a symphony of voices, a cacophony of laughter and heartache, secrets whispered over the rim of glasses and confessions spilled like the liquor that flowed so freely. I could hear the clinking of glass as they raised their drinks in celebration, toasting to the night that lay before them, filled with equal parts hope and despair.

I took a deep breath, inhaling the scent of whiskey and cigarettes that hung heavy in the air, mingling with the faint aroma of perfume and the unmistakable musk of human bodies pressed close together. The atmosphere was thick with desire and anticipation, an electric charge that sent shivers down my spine as I leaned against the worn wooden bar, feeling the grooves and indentations beneath my fingertips.

"Excuse me," I said to Belinda as she slid another drink across the counter to a waiting customer. "Can I get another whiskey, please?"

My voice quivered slightly as I spoke, betraying the tension that coiled within me like a serpent poised to strike.

"Sure thing, honey," she replied, her eyes meeting mine with a warmth that belied the shadows that danced across her face. As she moved to pour my drink, I couldn't help but notice the way her lithe body swayed gracefully, her every movement an intricate dance that defied the chaos that surrounded her. It was like she was the music itself, the life and soul of the bar, come to grace us all with her presence.

"Here you go," she said, placing the glass in front of me with a reassuring smile that seemed to say, 'I'll keep you safe.' I nodded my thanks, my fingers curling around the cool glass, a fleeting moment of solace before I surrendered myself to the whims of fate.

I took a slow sip of the amber liquid, feeling the burn as it slid down my throat, the warmth spreading through my chest like a beacon against the encroaching darkness. As I set the glass back down on the bar with a soft thud, I could feel the weight of the night pressing in around me, whispering of secrets yet to be uncovered and dangers that lurked just beyond my line of sight.

"Sometimes, you just need a little liquid courage," Belinda mused, her gaze drifting across the sea of faces that filled the room. "Especially in a place like this."

"I couldn't agree more," I replied, my thoughts echoing the sentiment as I looked around, waiting for that man whose eyes had promised me things his lips never said. He was nowhere in sight, so I sipped at my drink, waiting for the man who wouldn't ask me for forever because he didn't want that either. As the night stretched on, each moment drawing me closer to the reason I was really in this place, I knew that I would need every ounce of courage I could muster if I hoped to navigate the tangled web of mystery and desire that waited just beyond the threshold of the bar.

My heart drummed a nervous rhythm as my gaze swept over the lively crowd, searching for something to hold my attention, even if it was only for a little while. Asa hadn't appeared, so another man might do, if I could spot one that was unattached. The crowd dancing inside and outside the bar was entirely coupled up, though, with not a single man attractive enough for my tastes sitting on his own. The air hummed with the energy of dancers gliding with each other and with conversations and laughter, a symphony that both soothed and unsettled me.

"Robin," Belinda whispered, leaning closer, her breath warm against my ear. "Relax, love. You're glaring like you're about to cut the guy next to you to shreds."

Her words were well-intentioned but did little to quell the anxiety that coursed through me. I felt like a solitary island in a sea of people, a sore thumb that stuck out because of my singleness. I shouldn't be here. I should go back to my room, wait for sleep, for the nightmares, and start again tomorrow. Maybe the pills the doctor gave me back in New York would work for once?

And then, there he was, standing tall amidst the throng, an enigmatic figure who seemed to command the very air around him. Asa Kelley, clad in a beige suit that highlighted the powerful contours of his muscular frame, his disarming smile a beacon in the dimly lit room. My breath caught in my throat as my eyes met his, those piercing gray orbs that held within them the secrets of the universe. Or, at least, the promise of a good time, if I was so willing.

"Found him," I murmured, my voice barely audible above the clamor as I watched Asa weave through the crowd, his movements graceful yet predatory, a panther stalking its prey.

"Be careful, Robin," Belinda warned, her grip on my arm tightening briefly before she released me and returned to her duties behind the bar. "You don't know this town like I do. Or Asa, for that matter."

"I always am," I assured her, although doubts gnawed at the edges of my resolve.

As Asa neared, my pulse quickened, the anticipation

building like a crescendo within me. I tensed, readying myself for whatever might come next, my fingers gripping the edge of the worn wooden bar until my knuckles turned white.

"Evening, Robin," he said smoothly, the syllables rolling off his tongue like honey, a note of playful menace beneath his words. "It's a pleasure to see you again."

"Likewise," I replied cautiously, trying to keep my voice steady despite the way my heart raged within me the second he came close to me.

"Care for a dance?" Asa inquired, extending his hand towards me, an invitation and a challenge all at once.

"Lead the way," I acquiesced, my fingers brushing against his as I placed my hand in his, the electricity between us tangible and potent.

As we moved to the rhythm of the music, the rest of the world seemed to fade away, leaving only the two of us, locked in a dance that teetered on the edge of desire and danger. In that moment, I knew that he was coming back to my room with me, and I wasn't even a little bit worried about it. Asa would give me what I needed, what I had to have from him and only him. For tonight, anyway.

My heart raced as our gazes locked, the magnetic pull between us undeniable. I tried to remind myself of the danger he represented, but with every beat of my racing heart, I felt myself slipping further under his spell.

"Quite a lively place, this bar," Asa remarked casually, his gaze never leaving mine.

"New Orleans has its charms, and so does this bar," I replied, struggling to keep my voice steady as his hands slid along my body, guiding me as we moved in time with the music. "Besides, you're the one that lives here, you should know what to expect of the place."

"Ah, yes," he said with a knowing smile. "The music, the food, the people...and let's not forget the secrets."

"Secrets?" I asked, feigning ignorance even as my stomach twisted in knots.

"Every city has them, don't you think?" He leaned in closer, his warm breath brushing against my ear. "Some are more dangerous than others."

I swallowed hard, searching for a witty retort. "And what secrets do you think this city hides, Mr. Kelley?"

"Please, call me Asa," he insisted, his gray eyes sparkling with mischief. "As for the secrets...I believe there are those who would kill to protect them."

"Sounds rather ominous," I quipped, attempting to lighten the mood. But deep down, I knew he was right. The dark underbelly of New Orleans was all too familiar to a girl from New York City, and it seemed that Asa was intimately acquainted with it as well.

"Perhaps," he conceded, his grin never fading. "But that's what makes it so thrilling, isn't it? The allure of the unknown."

"Or perhaps it's just the whiskey talking," I countered, forcing a playful smirk. He twirled me around, taking my breath away in a gasp when he drew me back against his body, our lips close to pressing together, but not quite there yet.

"Could be," Asa agreed, a mischievous glint in his eye. "Or maybe it's just the company."

"Then maybe you should step away, Asa," I warned, although I couldn't help but feel a flutter of excitement at his words. "You might get burned."

"Ah, but where's the fun in that?" he retorted, and I couldn't suppress a smile.

As we continued our verbal dance, exchanging banter

and subtle innuendos, I found myself drawn deeper into the enigma that was Asa Kelley. I knew better than to trust him, after all, Belinda had warned me about him enough already. I suspected those warnings came because he was tied to the Irish Mafia that clawed to keep their control of their territory in the area, but couldn't prove it. For now, the warnings she'd made were a constant reminder of the danger he posed. And yet, as we shared knowing smiles and whispered encouragement, I couldn't help but wonder if there was more to him than met the eye.

The sultry melody of a saxophone drifted through the air, its seductive call weaving seamlessly with the low hum of whispered conversation and laughter. Caught in the spellbinding rhythm of the music, I found myself unable to resist the magnetic pull that drew me ever closer to Asa.

"Tell me something, Robin," he said, his voice a rich, velvety baritone that sent shivers down my spine. "What does freedom mean to you?"

I paused, the question catching me off guard. My eyes met his, searching for answers in the depths of his stormy gaze. But all I found was an enigmatic smile, as if he knew that he had rendered me speechless.

"Freedom?" I echoed, pondering the weight of the word. It seemed like such a distant dream, a hazy mirage on the horizon that always lay just out of reach. "I suppose...it means being untethered. Unbound by the chains of the past, free to chase the promise of tomorrow."

"Ah," he murmured, nodding thoughtfully. "A noble pursuit, indeed."

Our bodies gravitated towards each other, drawn together by an invisible force that defied reason or explanation. The warmth of his breath caressed my skin, sending goosebumps rippling across my flesh as the space between us dwindled to a mere whisper. I wasn't sure how much more of this I could stand, but I knew I was near my breaking point.

"I'm curious, Asa," I ventured, mimicking his words, my heart pounding in my chest. "What do you want out of life?"

"Me?" His fingers brushed against mine, an electrifying jolt shooting through our entwined hands. "I've always been a bit of a wanderer, a restless soul searching for a place to call home."

"Have you found it?" I asked, the intensity of his gaze threatening to consume me.

"Perhaps," he replied, his voice barely more than a whisper. "But there's still so much left to discover."

The urgency and desire that had been simmering beneath the surface of our encounter bubbled over, our conversation growing more intimate with each passing moment. Our laughter mingled with that of the people around us, the heady sensation of anticipation and longing intoxicating us both.

"Robin," Asa murmured, his breath hot against my ear. "I can't help but feel that our paths were destined to cross. That we were meant to find one another in this vast, infinite world."

"Destiny, huh?" I countered, a wry smile tugging at my lips. "That's a dangerous game you're playing."

"Ah, but who says I'm playing?" he challenged, his eyes sparkling with mischief. "Perhaps it's fate that brought us together."

"Or perhaps it's just a beautiful illusion," I whispered, my heart aching with the bittersweet knowledge that our time together was as transient as the fleeting notes of the saxophone's siren song. It's not like I was called here to attend a wedding or a birthday party, after all. I was in New

Orleans to find the man that murdered my sister and make sure he never took another breath. But that was for later. For now, Asa was willing and so was I.

The air around us seemed to thicken with desire, our stolen glances and lingering touches fueling a fire that raged within us both. Asa's fingers traced the curve of my jaw, his touch feather-light, setting my nerve endings ablaze with need.

"Is this what you want?" he asked, his voice husky and raw with emotion as our lips hovered a breath apart. I searched his eyes for any hint of hesitation, but all I found was the same yearning that echoed in my own heart.

"More than anything," I whispered, closing the gap between us.

Our mouths met in a searing kiss, a heady mixture of hunger and desperation. The taste of him, whiskey and cigarettes, mingling with the wild abandon of a man on the edge, was intoxicating. Our bodies pressed together, every point of contact sparking an electric current that sent shivers down my spine. We were two lost souls, seeking solace in one another's arms, as if somehow, we could escape the shadows that haunted us. But even as our passion threatened to consume us, a small voice in the back of my mind whispered words of caution. This man could be working with the same group that turned my sisters last days into a nightmare. Should I really give in to what I wanted to do?

"Wait," I gasped, pulling away from Asa and resting my forehead against his chest as I struggled to catch my breath. "I think I need a breath of fresh air. My head is spinning."

"How about I take you back to your place, instead" he murmured, the heat of his breath fanning over my skin, igniting goosebumps in its wake. "All I want right now is to lose myself in you, Robin."

"Are you sure?" I hesitated, torn between the undeniable pull I felt towards him and the knowledge that giving into our desires could have far-reaching ramifications. I wanted him, I wanted that wildness in him, I wanted to be as abandoned, yet controlled, as he seemed to be. Maybe I could sip a little bit of that from him, if I took him back to my room?

"More certain than I've ever been," he replied, his gray eyes holding mine captive. In that moment, I chose to surrender to the tide of passion that threatened to sweep me away, wondering if this was all because of that third whiskey I'd had, or if the all-consuming desire I felt for him was real.

4

Robin

"Come with me," I whispered, heading back to the bar to leave some money there for Belinda. She looked like she wanted to say something but when her eyes slid to Asa, she bit whatever it was back. I nodded at her, took his hand, and led him towards my motel room.

As we walked, the night air was heavy with the scent of magnolias and the occasional waft of spicy gumbo. The streets were mostly empty, the silhouettes of old buildings looming in the darkness like ghosts from another era. I fumbled with the key to my room, my hands shaking with both nervousness and anticipation. Asa watched me with a slight smirk, a knowing glint in his eyes that made my pulse race even faster.

Finally, the door opened with a soft click, and I stepped inside, beckoning him to follow. The room was small and sparsely furnished, with little more than a bed and a couple of chairs. But it was enough for what we had in mind.

Asa closed the door behind him, the sound echoing in the silence of the room. He took a step towards me, his hands reaching out to cup my face, his lips trailing a path of fire down my neck.

I moaned softly, my fingers tangling in his hair, clutching it as if I could bring him closer with the sheer force of my need. His hands slid down my body, one of them moving to cup my breast through the thin material of the black dress and equally black bra I had on, his thumb teasing my nipple to a hard peak. I arched my back, my body aching for more of his touch. I wanted to feel the solid warmth of him underneath my fingertips, wanted to feel him inside me, to know that he was as eager to clash together as we were.

The heat between us had become almost unbearable, and I knew there was only one thing that could blot out the fire that raged inside me. I needed to feel his body pressed against mine, to know that the unbridled desire we both felt was real.

He pulled at the silky material of my dress, easily sliding it off my body with a tug of his fingers. My fingers found the buttons of his shirt and I yanked it open, my body responding to Asa's need. I pushed the material away, pushing his suit jacket away with it as I did so. As soon as it was gone, he pulled me back to his body, tight against his bare chest.

Asa let out a groan as the cool air hit his exposed skin, but he didn't waste any time. Urgency and desire burned in his eyes, and I stepped back, allowing him a moment to take me in. I was wearing nothing but my boring white cotton panties and bra, and I could feel my heartbeat quicken at the hunger in his eyes as they roamed over me, leaving a trail of fire in their wake.

Asa didn't say anything, but the smolder in his gaze told

its own story, and I reached behind my back, undoing the clasp of my bra. I let it slide off my shoulders, freeing my breasts and I smiled softly at the way Asa's breath hitched in anticipation. I reached for the edges of my panties, sliding them down my legs, a shiver running through me at the raw hunger I could see in his eyes.

He reached out, running his hands up my thigh, his fingers grazing my skin, sending a jolt of electricity through me. It was as if he had somehow tapped into my innermost desires, and I couldn't get enough of him. I couldn't help but moan as my head fell back, his fingers still dancing on my skin, teasing me until I was gasping for air.

Asa kissed me, his mouth almost bruising in its intensity, his tongue taking me prisoner. I couldn't get enough of him, my hands sliding up and down his neck, over the hard muscles of his chest, before moving to the waist of his pants. There was no hesitation in his movements as I pushed them down, revealing the hard length of his cock. I hesitated for a moment, unsure of whether or not I should do this. It was one thing to give in to a moment's passion, but how far did I want to let this go?

"Do you want to taste it, Robin?" He asked, looking down at his cock then back up at me.

I made a strangled sound in the back of my throat, my eyes darkening with desire. Why did he turn me on so much? I thought. But before I could answer, I found his cock in my hands, I nearly gasped as I touched it. It was long and hard, poised and ready for action. The skin was soft, but the veins underneath were unmistakable, the sensation of them so alive and responsive against my fingers. I wrapped my hand around it, enjoying the way it filled my palm, the feel of the smooth skin over the hardness underneath.

"Yes, please," I said, moving to sit on the edge of the bed. "Let me taste you."

Asa's breath halted in his chest before he took a deep breath, his eyes narrowed on me, watching me as he moved towards me.

I'm far from a virgin and I know what I want. And right now? I want his cock in my hands, in my mouth, so I could make this man weak with desire. I wanted him trembling, begging for his release. A release only I could give him.

Asa stood in front of me, his breath coming in slow, even gasps. Carefully, I leaned forward, my tongue sliding out to taste the tip of his cock. I pulled back, the salty taste of him on my tongue, the creamy texture of his skin impossible to resist. I wrapped my lips around the head of his cock, sucking gently, and I could feel it swell against my tongue. A soft moan escaped my lips as I continued to savor the taste of him, the feel of him getting harder in my hands.

I wanted nothing more than to take him into my mouth, to taste him as he moaned, his body tightening with need for me. I slid my lips down his shaft, taking as much of him into my mouth as I could. A groan escaped his lips as my tongue continued to slide over him. I could feel his cock throbbing against my tongue, pulsing with the need he held inside, and I took delight in every moment of it. I sat back, savoring the taste of him, looking up at him with a dare in my eyes. Asa didn't say anything, he just looked at me, waiting, expectant, confident that I'd please him.

I licked my lips, then leaned forward again, slowly parting my lips, before taking the head into my mouth. Asa growled softly, his hands staying on my head, his fingers digging conspicuously into my flesh. I slid my mouth further down, taking more of him into my mouth, swallowing once again, before pulling back slowly, trying to ignore the sound of protest Asa made as I pulled away.

My hands slid over his hips and around to his ass, my fingers grabbing at him, pulling him towards me. I could taste his desire, feel it in my mouth, on my tongue. I wanted more of it, wanted to know how far I could push him before he couldn't stand it any longer. I needed this man. I needed to feel his body against mine, to know that we were as matched as the desire we both felt.

I took him into my mouth again, my tongue swirling over the head of his cock as I sucked and swallowed. I could feel Asa's hands move from my head, sliding over my back, my neck, until his fingertips were teasing the curve of my breasts, pulling and tugging at my nipples. I gasped as I slid my mouth down his length, moaning as his hands teased me, pinching my nipples gently.

I sucked faster, this time letting my tongue slide across the smooth skin, the tip of my tongue teasing the head of his cock. I did it again, savoring the sound of Asa's hoarse moan as I gave him more of my mouth. His cock slid across my lips, my tongue licked at it, and I took the head into my mouth again, sucking softly. My tongue slid over the tip again and again, sliding across his cock, touching everywhere I could reach, all the while his fingers digging into my scalp.

"Robin," he moaned, his voice strained. "You need...to stop...or you're going to make me come."

I smiled around his cock before I slid back up the shaft, only to slide back down once again, this time a little faster, taking him deeper into my mouth. Over and over I slid up and down, taking more of him each time.

I watched Asa's face, noting the way he breathed, the way his eyes spoke of desire that ran deeper than any I had ever seen. He was utterly lost in the pleasure I was giving him, his hips moving in time with my mouth, and soon, he was groaning almost as loudly as I was.

"Robin, I'm serious. If you want me to come in your mouth, I will, but, fuck, I want to be inside you when I come. But I don't mind coming all over that talented tongue of yours, if that's what you want," Asa warned, his eyes closed and his head back.

"Mmmm," I moaned around his cock, the vibrations sending a shiver through him.

I pulled back, but only far enough so I could look up at him, my tongue sliding out, tasting the tip of his cock again. I saw the sparkle in his eyes, and I smiled up at him, my hands sliding back up his hips, and I knew I had won. I had him right where I wanted him.

I slid back down his shaft, his cock hitting the back of my throat, before I pulled back, sliding up and down his length once again. I could feel his cock, swelling against my tongue, the heat of his desire only encouraging me to go faster, to take him in deeper. I sucked at him, my whole mouth devouring him, wanting to swallow him whole.

"You're going to make me come," he groaned with an urgency that only made me suck harder.

"Fuck, Robin, I'm going to come," he groaned, his fingers digging into my hair, tugging on the strands with just enough strength to make my nipples harden with pleasure. I like a little pain with my pleasure.

"Mmm," I moaned around his cock, sucking him harder. But Asa pulled away, taking my toy with him right before he flipped me over onto my stomach.

"You're fucking gorgeous, Robin," he whispered behind my ear just as his fingers dug into my ass. He let his right hand go, used it to slide down my ass and open my thighs.

His fingers slid forward to trace my opening, a finger teasing my clit, and I wanted nothing more in that moment than to feel him inside of me. I felt my hips jerk back to meet his hand, to try to force one of those teasing fingers inside of me.

"Fuck me," I begged, my voice hoarse, my body trembling.

Asa groaned, a deep sound that I felt rumbling in his chest as he leaned into me, his tongue coming out to lick at my earlobe. His hand came down on my ass, surprising me, but also, making me burn with surprised pleasure. I knew he understood me, the moment I saw him, I knew.

"You like it rough, Robin?" he asked, his voice low, his eyes dark with lust.

I nodded, incapable of lying to him at that moment. "Yes, please."

That was all he needed.

His hand came down again, harder, no doubt bruising me, but it felt so good, I didn't care. I needed this, I needed the shame of knowing I liked it.

Asa's hand came down again, the other coming up to palm my breast roughly, pushing my hair aside as he dropped his mouth to suck on my neck. The combination of pain and pleasure overwhelmed me, but he didn't stop there. The hand Asa had used to spank me now moved back between my legs, his fingers teasing my clit, his mouth against my neck. I gasped, wanting the pain back but then his gentle lips pulled back and he bit me, hard. He's going to mark me, I thought, and I didn't care.

Asa's fingers slid into me, just as his teeth sank into my flesh. I moaned, the sound echoed by Asa, and I pushed back into his hand. My hands gripped the pillow, my fingers curling into the fabric as he slid his fingers in and out of me, his teeth still firmly embedded in my neck. I knew I was going to bruise, but I didn't care. I wanted this. I wanted him.

"Asa," I moaned, my nails curling into the pillow, my body shaking with pleasure.

I was so close to coming, I only needed the whisper of a touch against my clit, and I would explode.

"Are you going to be a good girl for me, Robin? Are you going to get up and sit on my dick, let me fuck that sweet pussy of yours?" Asa asked as he rolled me over and pulled me up while he sat on the edge of the bed. "Turn around, back to me, and let me fill that hungry little pussy of yours."

I could only nod and do as I was told, hoping he'd let me finish if I did so. I needed to come so much. I gasped as his bare cock slid into me, opening me wide, filling me as I sank all the way down.

Asa groaned into my ear, his teeth seeking out new skin to bite as he teased at my nipples with one hand and my clit with the other. I started to move on him, grinding into him as my clit throbbed for more.

"Lean forward for me, my good little girl, show me what else I can have, later." Asa said, the hand that was once on my nipple now sliding around, pushing me forward a little. I thought I'd lose my mind when his fingers found my puckered entrance, pushing against my ass. I swallowed, knowing what he was about to do, but still unprepared when he forced two fingers into my ass. I moaned, my hips bucking back against his hand, grinding down on his cock, while the fingers of his other hand continued to work their magic on my clit.

"That's it, fuck my fingers, baby," he growled into my neck. His free hand came back up, his fingers pulling my hair tightly as he tugged at it.

I moaned, pushing back onto his hand as his fingers in my ass worked their way inside of me. His fingers were larger than I expected, but even as they stretched me, he worked them inside of me, pulling back out, and then in again, his finger brushing against my sweet spot. My whole body shuddered, then shook as Asa growled a hum of pleasure against my neck.

"Finger your clit, Robin, show me how you like it," Asa demanded, and I obeyed, too close to overwhelmed with him to do anything else. "And use that other hand on your nipples. We're going to send you into outer space, baby."

I cupped my right breast, the most sensitive of the two at the moment and clamped down hard on my nipple.

"Yes," I moaned, my eyes closing, my back arching as Asa's cock ground up into me. "Please, Asa, please."

"Please what, baby?" He asked, his teeth grazing my shoulder and I whimpered as he pushed his fingers into me.

I pushed back onto his cock, struggling to find words out of the pleasure and pain warring inside of me.

"Please, make me come. Make me come so hard," I begged, my whole body moving on him.

Asa gave me what I wanted, his fingers in my ass only working me harder and faster toward climax as he pounded into me. His hand on my hip pulled me back, forcing me onto his cock, the other hand only working me faster. I cried out, my finger pressed down on my clit as my body exploded. I came hard, my pussy clenching down on Asa's cock as my ass squeezed down on his fingers. My entire body shuddered as he filled me, as he bit down on my shoulder hard.

"Don't you dare stop moving, Robin," Asa growled as the pleasure began to ebb away, as sanity returned. I flexed my hips again, wanting to feel him come again, wanting to hear that groan of utter ecstasy that he made when he came.

"Fuck, Robin," Asa growled, his hips not as wild as they had been, he fucked into me a little slower, deeper, harder. When I came the second time, he was right there with me, coming hard into me, his cock throbbing with each pulse of his orgasm. I came down from my high, my hips moving slower, my body sated by him. His fingers pulled out of me, but he didn't let me go, not until he'd caught his breath. He moved then, pulling me up the bed with him and covering me with my own covers.

He cradled me close to him, my left leg over his hips as he stroked my face. I didn't really understand what was going on, but I was too tired to figure it out. I gave in to it, gave into him.

"Did I take you out of your head?" Asa asked, his finger sliding down my cheek.

I knew exactly what he meant. I nodded, not trusting my own voice.

"Good. Sleep now. Sleep and know you're safe. I won't let anything get to you." Asa said and I nodded. I was too tired to ask him what, or who, he meant, or to ask how he knew what I needed. It was enough that he was there. Maybe he was right, and for once, I was safe.

5

Asa

As I lay in bed, the moonlight streaming through the window, my thoughts drifted back to a time when life was simpler, before the chaos and darkness that would eventually consume me. It was as if the shadows of the past came alive, reminding me of what once was.

It was a hot, humid summer evening in New Orleans, the sun casting its golden glow over the city skyline. The faint scent of brine filled the air, carried in on the gentle sea breeze that ruffled my hair as I walked down the street. Laughter echoed from nearby homes, their windows open to let in the evening air. Somehow, the world seemed brighter back then, full of possibilities and innocence.

I wandered through the familiar streets of my old neighborhood, taking in the sights and sounds that had formed the backdrop of my youth. The shotgun houses were worn but still held a certain charm, their colorful window boxes overflowing with vibrant blooms.

Children played in the small park across from our house, their voices rising in excited chatter. I could hear the distant bark of a dog and the hum of cars passing by. The world felt alive, pulsating with energy and life.

My family's home stood proudly among its peers, its white paint pristine and inviting. The front yard was a lush, green oasis, carefully tended to by my father who took great pride in his gardening skills. I couldn't help but smile as I remembered the hours spent playing games and laughing with my siblings on that very lawn.

The memories washed over me like waves, each one bringing with it a sense of warmth and comfort. Yet, beneath the surface, there was something else, a darkness lurking, waiting to swallow me whole. A foreboding chill ran down my spine, a premonition of the tragedy that would soon befall us all.

As I continued to navigate the streets of my past, the sun dipped lower in the sky, casting long shadows that seemed to reach out toward me. The laughter and chatter slowly faded, replaced by the whispers of the wind as it wound its way through the trees.

The world around me began to change, the once-vibrant colors fading into muted tones of gray. I knew that, with each step I took, I was drawing closer to the darkness that would forever alter the course of my life. But for now, I allowed myself to bask in the warmth of those golden memories, a fleeting respite from the cold reality that awaited me.

The sun cast its final golden glow upon the peaceful suburban street as I sat on the porch steps, surrounded by my family. My mother, with her dark curls and warm smile, handed me a glass of cold lemonade while my father ruffled my hair affectionately.

"Thanks, Ma," I said, taking a sip as I watched my younger siblings playing catch in the front yard. Their laughter filled the air, a melody that eased the heaviness in my chest.

"Everything's going to be alright, Asa," my mother reassured me, her voice gentle yet firm. "We'll get through this together."

I nodded, feeling the weight of their support buoying me. We'd always been close, bound by an unbreakable love that saw us through the darkest times.

"Hey, Asa!" shouted my little brother, tossing the ball my way. I caught it effortlessly and threw it back, a small smile dancing on my lips. My sister, younger than both of us, played on the ground, clapping as we threw the ball.

"Nice catch!" my father praised, clapping his hands. His eyes sparkled with pride, and I felt a warmth spread through me knowing I could make him proud.

As we continued our game, I let the familiar rhythm lull me into a sense of security. But that peace was soon shattered by the sound of screeching tires and a cacophony of panicked voices.

"Get down!" my father yelled, pulling us all to the ground as bullets tore through the air, ripping apart the serenity of our once-peaceful home.

"Ma! Dad!" I screamed, my heart pounding wildly in my chest as the world around me dissolved into chaos. The warm embrace of my family had been replaced by the cold grip of terror, and I knew that nothing would ever be the same again.

Through the deafening hail of gunfire, I heard the guttural cries of my parents, my siblings' terrified whimpers. I tried to reach for them, but my limbs felt heavy, weighed down by a crushing sense of helplessness.

"Stay down, Asa," my mother gasped, her eyes filled with tears and desperation. "Please, just stay down."

But I couldn't stay down, not while my family was being torn apart before my very eyes. With a surge of adrenaline, I scrambled to my feet, searching for any way to protect the ones I loved.

"Run!" my father shouted, his voice barely audible above the chaos. "Get out of here, now!"

I hesitated, torn between my love for them and the instinct to survive. But as the gunfire intensified, leaving a trail of destruction in its wake, I knew there was no other choice. With one last glance at the broken bodies of my family, I turned and fled, their anguished cries echoing in my ears like the death knell of all that I had ever known and loved.

In the aftermath of that horrific night, I found myself crouched behind a rusted dumpster in an alleyway, my heart pounding like a jackhammer against my ribcage. The acrid stench of rotting garbage filled my nostrils, but it couldn't overpower the metallic tang of blood that clung to me like a second skin. My family's blood.

"Please," I whispered to whatever god might be listening. "Don't let them find me."

My fingers dug into the damp earth beneath me, seeking some semblance of stability as my world crumbled around me. Grief and guilt gnawed at my insides, a bitter cocktail that threatened to consume me whole. I should have stayed. I should have fought. But instead, I had listened to my father and run, leaving my family to die alone in that hellish storm of bullets.

"Who the fuck are you?" a voice snarled from the shadows, its suddenness jolting me from my despair. I glanced up to see a man emerging from the darkness, his salt-and-pepper hair slicked back and a hard gleam in his eyes. He wore an impeccably tailored suit, his stance exuding an air of authority that sent shivers down my spine.

"Leave me alone," I muttered, shrinking away from him. But he only smirked, clearly amused by my feeble attempt at defiance.

"Name's Declan O'Sullivan," he said, his voice as smooth as aged whiskey. "And you, boy, look like someone who could use a hand. You're Asa aren't you? My cousin Mary's boy?"

"I am, and no, I don't need your fucking help," I spat, my grief momentarily overshadowed by indignation. How dare this stranger think he could just waltz in and offer me help, as if that would make everything better?

"Suit yourself," he shrugged, turning to leave. And yet, as much as I hated to admit it, I knew that I couldn't survive on my own, not with the kind of enemies I had unwittingly made.

"Wait," I called out, cursing myself even as I did so. "Please."

Declan's smile widened, his eyes cold and calculating.

"That's more like it," he murmured, extending a hand toward me. "Welcome to your new life, Asa."

As I hesitated, weighing the cost of my pride against the price of survival, I couldn't help but wonder what kind of man this Declan O'Sullivan truly was. I'd heard whispers in the family about him, about how he was a bad man, the kind you didn't want to get tangled up with. Would he be my savior or my undoing? The answer remained elusive, shrouded in the darkness that had swallowed my family whole.

But as I finally grasped his outstretched hand, sealing

my fate with a touch, one thing became painfully clear: my life would never be the same again. And neither would I.

"Where do I even begin?" I whispered to myself, a bitter laugh escaping my lips as I stared at the ruins of what was once my family's home. I had buried them in the backyard, their final resting place marked by three simple crosses fashioned from wooden slats. My hands were still stained with dirt and sweat, reminders of the heart-wrenching task I had just completed.

It was then that I heard footsteps approaching, slow, deliberate, like the ticking of a clock counting down the seconds until my doom. As much as I wanted to run, to flee this nightmarish reality, I knew that escape was impossible. The enemies who had taken everything from me would not rest until they had claimed my life as well.

"Quite the mess you've got here," a deep voice drawled, and I felt a shiver run down my spine. Turning around, I found myself face-to-face with a man who seemed to embody danger itself. He was tall and broad-shouldered, with salt-and-pepper hair and piercing blue eyes that seemed to see straight through me.

"What do you want from me?" I demanded, my voice shaking slightly despite my best efforts to remain strong.

"Not a lot, boy," he replied, his tone nonchalant as if we were discussing the weather rather than standing amidst the wreckage of my life. "I just need you to do a few odd jobs for me, take care of a few things."

"Great," I muttered sarcastically. "I get to be your errand boy, huh?"

"At first." His gaze locked onto mine, and I felt a strange sort of electricity pass between us. "I want to help you. You're kin. We help each other out, right?"

"Help me?" I scoffed, my chest tightening with anger and disbelief. "What makes you think I need your help?"

"Call it intuition," Declan said, a faint smirk playing on his lips. "Or perhaps it's just experience. I've seen enough desperate men in my time to recognize the signs."

"Desperate?" I repeated, bristling at the implication. "I may have lost everything, but that doesn't mean I'm helpless."

"Of course not," he agreed, his voice dripping with feigned sincerity. "But it's clear you're out of your depth here, and the sharks are circling, Asa. You can either let them devour you whole or accept a lifeline when it's offered."

As much as I wanted to deny it, I knew he was right. My enemies would come for me again, and without protection, I wouldn't stand a chance. But could I truly trust this man, who seemed to hold power over so many others? The question gnawed at me, even as I realized I had no other choice.

"Fine," I said finally, gritting my teeth. "If you want to help me, then do it. But don't expect me to grovel at your feet."

"Wouldn't dream of it, lad," Declan replied, his grin widening. "But make no mistake, if you join our ranks, you'll be expected to pull your weight. We take care of our own, but loyalty goes both ways."

"Understood," I murmured, feeling the weight of my decision settle heavily on my shoulders. I had traded one form of danger for another, and only time would reveal whether I had made the right choice.

"Good," Declan said, clapping me on the back with a surprising gentleness. "Now, let's get started. There's much work to be done, and the sooner you learn the ropes, the better off you'll be."

As we walked away from the smoldering ruins of my past, I couldn't help but feel a mixture of trepidation and relief. I had stepped into the lion's den, and I'm not sure I was better off at all.

Months passed and I found myself quickly becoming... busy. The smell of stale whiskey and cigarette smoke clung to the air in the dimly lit pub, a place where secrets were whispered and deals were made in shadowy corners. I clutched a glass in my hand, nervously swirling the amber liquid as I observed the room. Since joining Declan's ranks, my life had taken on a new meaning, one filled with danger and uncertainty.

"Oi, Asa!" a rough voice called from across the room. It was Seamus, one of Declan's right-hand men. "Quit daydreamin'. We've got work to do."

"Right," I muttered under my breath, downing the rest of my drink before following him through the back door and into the alleyway. The cold, damp air hit me like a slap to the face, but I didn't flinch. This was my reality now, this world of violence and deception.

We arrived at our destination, an old warehouse near the docks, and I could feel my pulse quicken. Seamus had informed me that we were here to collect a debt from someone who had crossed Declan. As we entered the dimly lit building, I couldn't help but wonder if I was ready for such a task.

"Remember," Seamus said gruffly as he handed me a bat, "we're here to send a message. You follow my lead, and you'll be fine."

I nodded, gripping the cold metal in my hand tightly as

we approached the unfortunate debtor. He was bound to a chair, eyes wide with terror as they flicked between Seamus and me. Part of me wanted to look away, to pretend that I wasn't a part of this brutal world. I was still just a kid, wasn't I? But another part of me, the part that longed to avenge my family and cling to the protection Declan provided, urged me to step forward and prove myself.

"Please," the man whimpered, "I'll get you the money. I just need more time."

"Time's up," Seamus growled, and with a sickening crack, he swung his bat into the man's leg.

The sound echoed through the warehouse, and I felt bile rise in my throat. But as I looked at the mangled limb, something inside me snapped. I thought of my family, their bodies broken and lifeless, and how Declan had been there for me. And so, I raised the bat and brought it down on the man's other leg, ignoring his screams of agony.

"Good lad," Seamus said approvingly, slapping me on the back. "You've got a taste for this now, huh?"

"Let's just get this over with," I replied, swallowing hard as we continued our brutal task.

Later that night, as I lay in bed, my thoughts raced. The memory of the man's pained cries haunted me, and I couldn't shake the feeling that I was betraying my family by aligning myself with Declan and the Irish mafia. But what choice did I have? It was either this or face the world alone, vulnerable to those who sought to do me harm.

I closed my eyes, trying to push away the guilt and regret that weighed heavily on me. As I drifted off to sleep, I couldn't help but wonder whether I would ever be able to reconcile my past with the twisted path I now walked. Or if I would forever be lost in the darkness, tethered to Declan O'Sullivan and the dangerous world he ruled.

Months had passed since that fateful night, and my involvement in the Irish mafia only deepened. The more time I spent under Declan's wing, the more I found myself drawn to him. He was a complicated man, full of contradictions and capable of both cruelty and kindness. But it was the moments when he showed me his vulnerable side, when he let down his guard and allowed me to see beneath the hardened exterior, that truly solidified our bond.

"Looks like we've got another shipment coming in tonight," Declan said one evening as we sat in his office, the dimly lit space filled with the scent of whiskey and cigars. "I need you to make sure everything goes smoothly."

"Of course," I replied, my voice steady despite the unease that churned within me. With each new task, each new compromise I made, I felt as though I was losing a piece of myself. And yet, I couldn't bring myself to walk away from this life, from the man who had given me purpose and a place to belong.

"Good lad," Declan murmured, his dark eyes flicking up to meet mine. There was something in his gaze, an unspoken understanding that seemed to say he knew the sacrifices I was making for him, for this organization. It was in these moments that I felt an almost desperate loyalty to the man, a willingness to do whatever it took to protect him and the empire he had built.

That night, as we stood on the docks waiting for the shipment to arrive, I couldn't shake the feeling that something was wrong. My instincts had been honed through years of loss and hardship, and they screamed at me now to be on guard. It wasn't long before my suspicions were confirmed, as gunfire erupted around us, rival gang members appearing out of the shadows.

"Get down!" Declan shouted, pushing me behind a stack

of crates as bullets whizzed through the air. I felt a surge of adrenaline, my heart hammering in my chest as I clutched my own gun tightly.

"Stay here," I whispered to Declan, knowing that it was my duty to protect him, no matter the cost. My breath came in shallow gasps as I moved between cover, taking down our attackers one by one. With each shot, each life I took, I could feel the weight of my actions bearing down upon me, the guilt and regret threatening to swallow me whole.

When the last of our enemies lay dead or dying on the ground, I stumbled back to where Declan was hiding, my hands shaking from the aftermath of violence. He looked at me with an intensity that made my breath catch, his eyes full of gratitude and something deeper, something I couldn't quite name.

"Thank you," he said softly, his voice barely audible above the sound of the waves crashing against the shore. "I owe you my life."

"Declan, I...I don't know how much longer I can do this," I admitted, my voice trembling. "The things I've done, the people I've hurt...I feel like I'm losing myself."

"Sometimes we have to lose ourselves in order to find our true purpose," he replied, his hand gripping my shoulder firmly. "And sometimes, we have to make sacrifices for the ones we care about. But remember this, Asa, you're not alone. You have me, and together, we'll rule this entire filthy fucking world. It can all be ours."

As we stood there on the blood-stained docks, the moon casting an eerie glow over the scene, I knew that Declan was right. For better or worse, our fates were intertwined, and no matter the emotional toll it took on me, I couldn't imagine my life without him by my side.

Months had passed, and my life within the Declan's

organization deepened. The line between who I once was and who I had become blurred, fading like mist in the morning sun. Declan's constant presence was both a comfort and a reminder of the life I'd chosen, one that promised no escape.

As I sat in a dimly lit room, watching the shadows dance on the walls, I thought about what it meant to fully embrace this world. The darkness that consumed me threatened to extinguish the last remaining embers of the man I used to be. A knock on the door broke my reverie.

"Come in," I called, steeling myself for whatever task lay ahead.

Declan entered, his face grave. "There's been a complication, Asa. Our rivals are moving against us tonight. We need to make a stand."

A cold sweat prickled at the nape of my neck, but I nodded, accepting the consequences of my choices. "What do you need me to do?"

"Be by my side," he said simply, his eyes never leaving mine. "Together, we'll protect what's ours."

As we prepared for the impending confrontation, I felt a mix of dread and determination coursing through my veins. This would be the night I truly proved my loyalty, not just to Declan, but to the organization as a whole.

The air was thick with tension as we stood before our enemies, their sneers and taunts echoing in the cold night air. But I refused to let fear take hold. I looked to Declan, standing tall beside me, and knew that I would do anything to protect him.

"Remember, Asa," he whispered, his voice steady and low, "you're one of us now. Show them what you're made of."

As the first shots rang out, time seemed to slow. With every pull of the trigger, every life I took that night, I felt a piece of myself slip away, replaced by an unyielding determination to survive. And as the last of our enemies fell, I knew I had made my choice, I was no longer just Asa Kelley; I was a member of the Irish mafia, and there was no turning back.

"Good work, Asa," Declan said, his voice tinged with both pride and sorrow. "You've proven yourself tonight."

"Thank you, Declan," I replied, my voice hollow, the weight of my actions settling heavily upon me.

The present day came crashing in like a tidal wave, washing away the memories of that blood-soaked night. I stood in front of the mirror, staring at the man who had become a stranger to himself.

"Are you all right?" Robin's soft voice drifted from behind me, her concern palpable.

"Yeah," I lied, my reflection betraying the turmoil within. "Just lost in thought."

I couldn't help but wonder how my past would continue to haunt me, and what impact it would have on the present. With each passing moment, the truth loomed closer, casting its shadow over everything I held dear.

I stood by the window of her motel room, the warm sunlight filtering through the curtains and casting shadows across the room. The faint laughter of late-night revelers walking by outside drifted in like memories of a life I once knew. Robin's soft breathing filled the silence beside me as she slept, her chest rising and falling in peaceful rhythm. I watched her for a moment, my heart swelling with both affection and regret.

"Things could have been different," I whispered to myself, my voice barely audible. The words tasted bitter, a reminder of the choices I had made and the life I had left behind. I leaned against the windowsill, my gaze drifting over the quiet neighborhood beyond. It was a world that now felt foreign to me, tainted by the darkness of my past.

"Is everything all right?" Robin murmured, stirring from her slumber. Her eyes fluttered open, seeking mine with concern.

"Everything's fine," I reassured her, forcing a smile. "Just thinking."

"About what?" She propped herself up on one elbow, her curiosity piqued.

"About the past," I admitted hesitantly. "And how it affects the present."

"Sometimes the past can't be changed," Robin said gently, reaching out to touch my arm. "But it doesn't mean we can't learn from it or try to make amends."

"Sometimes amends aren't enough," I replied, my thoughts consumed by memories of Declan and the Irish mafia, a life I had willingly embraced, despite the cost.

"Maybe not," she conceded, "but it's a start."

"Is it?" I questioned, my voice laced with doubt. "Can someone truly escape their past?"

"Perhaps not entirely," Robin mused, her fingers tracing idle patterns on my skin. "But we can choose how much power it holds over us."

"Even when our past actions have consequences that reach into the present?" I asked, my thoughts heavy with the weight of my own guilt and regret.

"Especially then," she asserted, her gaze meeting mine with unwavering conviction. "That's when it's most important to face those consequences and try to make things right."

I stared at her, marveling at her strength and resilience in the face of adversity. She was so full of good it made me ache to protect her, to hide her from the world. She was a reminder that there was still goodness worth fighting for.

"Maybe you're right," I conceded, taking a deep breath as I wrestled with the demons of my past. "Maybe there is a way to find redemption, even in the darkest corners of our lives."

"Of course there is," Robin affirmed, her voice soft but resolute. "You just have to be ready to fight for it."

As we lay there, our fingers entwined and our hearts beating in unison, I couldn't help but think how far I had come from that fateful night when everything changed. The path before me remained uncertain, fraught with danger and the ever-present specter of my past. But Robin have me a new reason to hope. She'd come into my life quietly, a slow smile and wary eyes telling me she'd been hurt, badly, before. After our first real night together, I knew I had something worth holding onto, a reason to keep fighting, despite the shadows that threatened to swallow us whole.

6

———————

Robin

I stared into my lukewarm cup of coffee, the dark liquid swirling like a vortex of unanswered questions and doubt. My thoughts kept drifting back to the previous night's encounter with Asa Kelley, the man who had managed to infiltrate my thoughts no matter how hard I tried to keep him out of them. My response to him last night had come with an intensity I'd never experienced before, as if he were a blazing bonfire in the midst of a cold, desolate winter's night. But the heat that radiated from him also threatened to consume me, because Asa wasn't just any man. I suspected he had connections to the organization that tore my family apart.

"Damn it," I muttered under my breath, gripping the ceramic mug tightly as if trying to contain my conflicting emotions. My mind wandered back to the way he held me, his arms wrapped around me like a protective barrier, yet there was a vulnerability to his touch that intrigued me. A small part of me wanted to believe that Asa was different, that he could be my anchor in this chaotic world. But could I really trust him? Was I fooling myself by entertaining the idea of letting him into my life any more than he already was?

My chest tightened as I contemplated the potential consequences of pursuing a relationship with Asa. I couldn't shake the feeling that getting involved with him would invite danger, not only to myself but to my sanity. And yet, something deep within me longed to explore the depths of this enigmatic man, to uncover the secrets hidden behind his piercing eyes. It was a temptation that was almost impossible to resist.

"Robin, are you okay?" The concerned voice of Belinda pulled me from my reverie.

"Uh, yeah, I'm fine," I replied, forcing a smile onto my face. "Just...thinking."

"About Asa?" she asked cautiously, her emerald eyes narrowing in suspicion.

"Maybe," I admitted, taking a deep breath and releasing it slowly. "I just...I don't know if getting involved with him is worth the risk, you know?"

"Robin, I can't make your choices for you, but Asa? He's trouble, I've told you that before," Belinda said softly, her voice tinged with sadness.

Her words resonated within me, stirring up a whirlwind of emotions that left me feeling both exhilarated and terrified. I was confused by the connection I felt with Asa, and I have to uncover the truth about my family's tragedy. Could I do that with him by my side? Or would I just be putting myself into the hands of the devil. Had I already done that? Was it too late to turn back now?

The air was thick with tension as I stared out the window, watching the raindrops race down the glass like tears of sorrow. My heart felt heavy in my chest, burdened by the uncertainty of what lay ahead. The smell of damp earth and rain-soaked streets filled my nostrils, a bittersweet reminder of the fragile nature of life.

"Robin, remember to breathe," Belinda whispered, her hand gently squeezing mine in reassurance.

"Right," I murmured, my eyes still fixed on the dismal world outside.

As if summoned by my thoughts, Asa stepped into the bar, the atmosphere shifting palpably with his presence. His disarming smile warmed me from within, while his eyes seemed to promise that he saw only me. He moved with an effortless grace, every step carrying the weight of a man who knew too well the danger that lurked beneath the surface of our lives.

"Hey, Robin," he said softly, his voice sending shivers up my spine. "I hope I'm not interrupting."

"No, not at all," I replied, unable to tear my gaze away from him. It was as if we were magnets, drawn inexorably towards one another despite the risks that lay between us.

"Mind if I join you?" he asked, his eyes never leaving mine as he came up to the bar.

"Please do," I managed to say, my heart pounding wildly in my chest.

Asa took a seat beside me, his muscular frame radiating warmth that seeped into my very bones. My breath hitched as our fingers brushed against each other, a jolt of electricity passing between us. We were fire and ice, passion and caution, locked in a dance as old as time itself.

"Robin," he murmured, his voice tugging at something deep within my soul. "I hope you're having a good day?"

"It's been alright," I replied, not giving away that I've been sitting at this bar for hours, wondering what to do next. Find another motel and avoid Asa before I formed some kind of emotional attachment I didn't want, or stay and find out anything he might know about my sister and who'd destroyed her and my entire world with her?

"Had dinner?" He asked, motioning to Belinda to get him a drink. She settled a bottle of cold beer in front of him, watching us both for a moment before she stepped away.

"No, but I'm alright for now. You?" I asked, my voice trembling with emotion, with the things I wanted to ask but couldn't. Not yet.

"No, I haven't eaten yet today," he replied, his eyes locked on mine with unwavering intensity. "Want to go out for something later?"

"Yeah, I think I would," I replied, making a choice, for better or worse. As the rain continued to fall outside, I knew there'd be a price to pay, one way or another. I'd learn to live with it, eventually.

The door swung open, and a cacophony of laughter and conversation spilled in as people headed for a table in the corner of the bar. Neon signs advertising various libations cast their garish glow over the patrons who filled every nook and cranny of the dimly lit space. Music played from a jukebox in the corner, the sultry strains of bluesy music weaving through the air like tendrils of smoke. The atmosphere was alive with energy, an electric pulse that seemed to vibrate beneath my skin.

"The place is busy," Asa said, his charismatic presence drawing admiring glances from the other patrons as they made their way toward the crowded bar. I only had eyes for Asa, though, feeling the familiar magnetic pull that drew me towards him even as I fought against it. The faint scent of his cologne wafted through the air, teasing my senses and making my heart race.

"Cheers," he said, raising his bottle in a toast. I hesitated for a moment before clinking my mug against his, the sound echoing ominously in my ears.

"Cheers," I echoed, taking a sip and trying to steady my trembling hands.

"Let me ask you a personal question, Robin," he began, his eyes searching my face as if trying to uncover the secrets hidden within. "What's your favorite memory from childhood?"

I couldn't help but smile at the totally unexpected question.

"There was a small park near our house," I began, the melancholic tone in my voice betraying the bittersweet nature of the memory. "My mom used to take us there every Sunday, and we'd have picnics under a big oak tree."

"Sounds nice," Asa replied, his gaze never leaving mine. "Mine is similar, actually. My family had a boathouse, out in the bayou near Houma, and we'd spend our summers there fishing and swimming."

"Seems like we both have a penchant for simpler times," I said, a small laugh escaping my lips. It felt strange to be discussing something so innocent with a man who was anything but.

"Sometimes, I think we all long for those days when life was less complicated," Asa mused, taking another sip of his drink before continuing. "But you can't escape your past, can you?"

"No," I agreed, my voice barely above a whisper. "No, you can't."

Our conversation continued, the tone changing, the whispered words becoming more flirtatious. The banter between us grew more intense as the night wore on and I switched from coffee to beer. We danced around the subject of our shared night together, neither of us willing to acknowledge the dangerous game we were playing.

"Robin," Asa murmured at one point, his voice low and enticing. "You know, I've always believed that fate has a way of bringing people together for a reason."

"Maybe," I replied, my heart pounding in my chest as the weight of our unspoken words pressed down upon me. "But sometimes, fate can be cruel."

"True," he conceded, his eyes darkening with an emotion I couldn't quite decipher. "But perhaps, in the end, it's up to us to determine whether we're victims or survivors."

I frowned at that, not liking it, but seeing the truth in what he'd said. As the night wore on and the bar grew more crowded, I found myself torn between the desire to flee from Asa's magnetic presence and the need to stay by his side. The uncertainty and unease that filled me only intensified as I struggled to reconcile the man before me with the enigma he represented.

"Are you ready to go?" Asa asked eventually, his hand reaching across the bar to cover mine. I hesitated for a moment before nodding, unable to resist the lure of his touch any longer.

"Lead the way," I whispered, surrendering to whatever the night, and Asa might bring my way.

As we settled at the diner near my room, the pulsating beat of the music and the laughter in the air from the bar's patrons seemed like a distant echo. Asa led me to a booth and I sat down, wondering if he'd end up in my bed again in an hour or two. Or would he leave me to wrestle with my nightmares, nightmares I didn't have last night, with him there beside me. He'd been gone when I woke up, but that was fine. I slept through the night, at least.

We ordered food, but I couldn't tell you what we ate. Something with cheese, maybe, or perhaps steak with a baked potato. I don't know because I don't remember eating it. I was wound up with anticipation. I wanted him to come back to my room with me, but I hated that I wanted it. I hated that I wanted him. We left after Asa paid, headed in no clear direction. There was something about the way Asa walked that exuded confidence, shoulders broad, head held high, every step measured and deliberate. I couldn't help but be drawn to him, even though the shadows of his past loomed over us like an ever-present specter.

"Are you sure about this?" he asked, pausing as we reached my door. His voice was laced with concern, as if giving me one last chance to reconsider. After all, we couldn't exactly call the night before anything like gentle lovemaking. Was I prepared to go through that maelstrom again? I think I was.

"Nothing in life is certain," I replied, taking a deep breath, the scent of his cologne infiltrating my senses, making me shiver with anticipation. "But sometimes, we have to take risks to get the answers we seek."

He nodded solemnly, unlocking the door and guiding me inside. The dim lighting cast a warm glow on the room, the soft hum of the city outside filtering through the windows. Our surroundings seemed to mirror the uncertainty and unease that clouded our minds, yet the magnetic pull between us refused to be denied.

Our lips met tentatively at first, as if testing the waters of the unknown all over again. But soon, the dam broke, and the force of our passion surged forward without restraint. His hands roamed my body, eliciting shivers down my spine as they trailed along the curve of my hips, the small of my back.

"God, Robin," he whispered into my ear, his breath hot and urgent. "I've been wanting this all fucking day."

"Then show me," I urged, my voice trembling with desire as I pressed myself against him.

Asa's touch was both tender and rough, a paradox that sent my mind spiraling into chaos. Every caress felt like fire against my skin, every kiss a desperate plea for more. We lost ourselves in each other, the rest of the world fading away, until there was nothing left but the intensity of our connection. I felt his touch as he dragged the simple dark blue wrap dress up my thighs before he found the tie that would open the panels. It slid from my shoulders revealing the black lace bra and panties I wore. He inhaled slowly, deliberately as he looked at me, taking in my body.

When his eyes came back up to mine, they were dark with desire and the promise of more to come. "I've thought about you sucking my dick all day long. How pretty you were with your lips wrapped around me, sucking me like you'd found your favorite candy."

"Maybe I have, Asa," I replied boldly, undoing my bra and stepping out of my panties. "But, as I recall, you wanted to fuck me more than you wanted your dick sucked."

He smirked at me then, his eyes alight with amusement. "There was that little nugget in my brain too, how it felt to fuck you, have you coming all over me."

"And which do you want the most tonight, Asa?" I asked, wanting him, not even thinking about the nightmares now. In 24 hours, he'd become an addiction, and I couldn't seem to help myself.

"I want both," he replied, growling the words to me as he stalked closer, his fingers lingering at my jaw. "But honestly, swallowing your moans while I'm inside you is the one that's been driving me crazy all day."

His eyes darkened as he considered my naked body. I shivered at the thought of what was to come, but also at the thrill of his desire for me. I stepped away from the dress and approached him, reaching out to touch his rock-hard cock through his pants. He groaned softly as I stroked him, an echo of the soft moan I made feeling the heat and thickness of him beneath my fingers.

"Are you sure you're up for it, Robin?" he asked, his voice hoarse with need. "I don't want to hurt you."

I smiled at him, running my fingers through his hair. "You won't hurt me, Asa. I'm all in."

"Don't forget I asked you that, later," Asa said softly, pulling me to his body. His lips crashed to mine, his tongue sliding past my lips to tangle with mine. His fingers grasped at my ass with a bruising grip, and I didn't care if he was tied up with the Irish mafia, or if he was a shoe salesman, I wanted those little points of pain to continue until he made me black out with pleasure.

7

———

Robin

"Hold on, just a second," Asa said, backing up to remove the white polyester shirt and black pants he had on, kicking his shoes away somewhere in the direction I'd kicked mine. I almost felt cold, despite the humid heat outside, so when he came back to me, I savored the heat of his body against mine. "I want you so much, Robin."

"Then have me, Asa," I whispered, my hands going down to grasp his length in my hand, to stroke him as those beautiful gray eyes closed and he lost himself in my touch.

I went down on my knees before him, my trembling hands reaching out to cradle his balls, my tongue tracing a path up the veiny length of his cock. I heard his low growl, a clear indication of the pleasure I was giving him, and I swirled my tongue around the head, savoring the salty taste of his precum. I hummed gently, the vibrations traveling through his body, making him shudder with desire.

Asa's hands gripped my hair, threading through the

strands as he thrust his hips forward, driving himself deeper into my mouth. I took him all in, feeling him hit the back of my throat, the sensation of his girth filling me, leaving me breathless. I gagged slightly, but he held me still, fucking my face slowly, gently, but with clear intent. He wasn't going to stop this time. That was good because I didn't want him to.

His fingers tightened in my hair, guiding me deeper, and I choked on his cock, but I didn't mind. I wanted this. I needed this. Asa's thrusts became more intense, his breath coming in ragged gasps. I could sense he was close, and I wanted to make him come.

I sucked and licked, my lips pressing against his shaft, setting a rhythm that had him moaning my name. His grip on my hair tightened, and I knew he was about to cum. I pulled back slightly and swirled my tongue around the head of his cock, the salty tang of his precum making my mouth water.

Asa shuddered violently, his hips bucking as his release flooded my mouth. I swallowed it down, savoring the taste and feeling the warmth of his seed filling my mouth. When he was finished, he slowly pulled himself from my mouth, his breath ragged.

As I stood up, my knees weak and wobbly, I could hear the sound of our hearts pounding in unison. Our lips met in a deep, passionate kiss as our tongues danced together, tasting the salty remnants of his release.

"That was incredible," I whispered against his lips, my voice shaking from the intensity of our encounter.

Asa's arms wrapped around me, pulling me close. "You're the only one who has ever made me feel this way."

His voice was soft, filled with genuine emotion that made my heart flutter.

"What way, Asa?" I asked, curious.

"Like I want to wrap you in velvet and keep you all to myself." He whispered, kissing me gently.

"I don't need protecting, Asa. I need fucking. I want you to come inside me," I said, needing him to fill me completely.

"Of course," he replied, his voice rough with desire.

He guided me to the bed, where I lay down on my back, spreading my legs wide and inviting him in. Asa moved between my legs, but it was his face that he pressed to my folds, his tongue that slid into the crease to lick up the evidence of just how much I wanted him. It was his lips that wrapped around my clit and sucked, making me shudder harder when he slid two fingers inside of me.

I clutched at the bed sheets as sensations surged up, straight into my brain, making me gasp uncontrollably.

Asa continued to pleasure me with his lips, his tongue dancing around my erect clit, moving it in circles and driving me wild. My hips bucked under his skillful touch as he slid his fingers deeper inside me, hitting my G-spot and causing a wave of pleasure to wash over me. My breaths came out in short gasps as I felt the tension building.

Asa's soft thumb brushed against my clit, sending an electric shock through my body. I could feel the tension in my muscles, the burning desire building up inside me. My back arched, and I threw my head back, letting out a loud moan as the release took over. My body shook violently as wave after wave of pleasure washed over me, each one stronger than the last.

My muscles clenched around Asa's fingers, and I felt him withdraw them, leaving me feeling empty and wanting more. I opened my eyes on the verge of pleading with him, but he was grinning up at me.

"You want fucking, or you want this, Robin? Which is it

to be?" Asa asked, his thumb teasing at my clit again, making it hard to think.

"I'm so close, Asa, I just want to come," I panted out, reaching for him, making my decision.

Asa's cock was going to drive me wild. I could feel the tension in my muscles, the excitement bubbling just below the surface. I spread my legs wider, inviting him in.

He didn't need to be told twice and moved to position himself at my entrance. A loud groan filled the air as he pushed into me, and I don't know which of us made it, or if it was both. Asa went deep with his thrusts as he moved slowly at first, before picking up his pace. Each thrust was deliberate, each movement a signal of his desire for me. I wrapped my legs around his waist, pulling him deeper into me, feeling him fill me completely.

Our bodies moved in sync with each other, both of us knowing intuitively what the other needed most. His hands gripped my waist roughly, painfully, filling me with little bursts of glee as the pain turned to fierce pleasure, pulling me closer to him with each thrust. His gray eyes locked onto mine, and I could see the passion and desire in them.

"Asa, oh, Asa," I moaned, my voice a mix of pleasure and pain. I could feel every inch of as he thrust into me, his hard abs moving with each thrust. I wanted to lick every single each of him, but maybe I'd save that for later.

Asa moved, rolling me on top of him, his hands still gripping my hips tightly.

"I love seeing you above me." He said, his breath catching in his throat. "Come down here, where I can get to those delicious nipples of yours."

I leaned over happily, letting him suck at my nipples while my hand moved down, down to my clit. I needed to come so desperately I couldn't wait. And I wanted to come with Asa deep inside of me.

I moved my hips up and down, riding his cock with desperate intensity, feeling the friction between us, the heat building, the passion, the wild craziness of it, and the need. His hands gripped my ass tightly, pulling me closer to him, driving himself deeper into me, and I moaned his name as he filled me completely. Our bodies moved with an electric intensity, the sound of our hips slapping together filling the room.

As I stroked myself, he moaned, watching me in awe. "You're so beautiful, Robin. I want to make you come so hard you forget your own name."

My body trembled at his words, and I began to pant and moan. Asa reached up, his hands gripping my hips, pulling me closer to him. His cock was throbbing inside me, and with each thrust, I could feel the pleasure building.

"Asa, I'm so close," I gasped, my voice breaking. His fingers dug into my hips, and he thrust harder into me, his breath ragged.

"Take me with you, Robin," he groaned, his fingers sliding around to my ass, to tease the entrance there. He knew I loved that. He gathered some of my juices before he slid the finger back to my ass, pushing into me, deeper, and deeper, until the first knuckle was deep inside of me.

"I need you so bad," I whispered, my voice shaking with raw desire. "I need to feel you come inside me."

Asa's grip on me tightened, his thrusts becoming more intense, that finger in my ass pushing deeper, driving me wild with need. His breath was ragged, his eyes locked onto mine, and I knew he was close.

"I'm going to come," he growled, his voice raw with desire.

I clamped my legs around his waist offering him my breasts again. He took one and clamped down tightly with his teeth, shocking me, completing me, as I cried out his name.

The pleasure that rocked through me made me see stars, stole my breath, and I think I might have actually died as my body curved and writhed on him.

"Fuck, that's beautiful," Asa ground out, thrusting up into one final time as he came again, his body shuddering beneath mine. I felt my walls milking every last drop of his essence from him and sighed with satisfaction.

"Robin," Asa panted moments after I collapsed beside him, my leg thrown over his, my head on his chest, our breaths ragged and uneven. "Whatever happens next, just remember, I'm here for you."

I nodded, tracing my fingers along the contours of his face, trying to commit every detail of the moment to memory. In that moment, I knew that my decision to pursue whatever this was with Asa might have far-reaching consequences, both for myself and whatever came next for me. But I also understood that it was a risk I had to take, driven by the hope that he could help me uncover the truth about my family's tragedy.

"Thank you, Asa," I whispered, resting my head on his chest. "For everything."

As I lay beside Asa, wrapped in the cocoon of his embrace, I couldn't help but wonder if I was making a terrible mistake by getting involved with him. The risks were immense, but so to were the potential rewards. Asa could be my way to get to the man who killed my sister. Or he might be setting a trap for me.

"Hey," Asa said, brushing a strand of hair from my face. "You're a million miles away. Did something happen?"

I hesitated, unsure how to express the whirlwind of emotions coursing through me. "I just...it's been a long day, that's all."

"Take all the time you need," he replied, his expression a mix of understanding and sadness. "But remember that I'm here for you, no matter what."

"Thank you," I whispered, grateful for his support despite the turmoil within me.

As we lay there, our bodies entwined amidst tangled sheets, the shadows of doubt and uncertainty that had consumed me began to dissipate ever so slightly. But still they lingered at the edges of my consciousness, a nagging reminder of the danger that lurked beneath the surface of our newfound connection.

THE SOFT GLOW of the morning sun filtered through the curtains, casting a warm, golden light across the room. I lay there, Asa's arm draped protectively over me, and for a brief moment, our world seemed almost perfect. But deep down, I knew that this illusion of safety was as fragile as the gossamer threads that held it together.

"Robin," Asa murmured, stirring beside me. "What's on your mind?"

"Nothing," I replied, forcing a smile as I turned to face him. But even as I said the words, I couldn't shake the growing sense of foreboding that gnawed at my insides like a relentless tide. "I think I just need some coffee and breakfast."

"Come on," he urged gently, his thumb tracing circles on my skin. "I can practically hear the gears turning in that pretty head of yours."

"Alright," I sighed, deciding that perhaps voicing my fears would help alleviate them. "I'm just...I came down here to find some answers."

"Answer about what?" he asked, his eyes searching mine.

"About some things that happened to my family," I whispered, the weight of their memory bearing down upon me like an anchor. "And about people you may or may not know."

The words hung heavy between us, shadowed by the things I'd left unsaid and what I'd really meant.

"Robin," Asa began, his voice firm but gentle. "I won't let anything happen to you. You have my word."

"Your word...," I repeated, the syllables ringing hollow in my ears. How could I trust the word of a man who could be deeply entwined with the very organization responsible for the deaths of my mother and sister?

"Robin," Asa said, his voice laced with concern. "Talk to me. What's going on?"

"I need to know the truth, Asa," I whispered, my heart pounding in my chest as I trusted him with words that could get me killed. "About my sister, about the girls that disappear down here because of some guy that people don't want to talk about...about everything."

"Robin," he sighed, the weight of my words etched onto his face. "I'll help you in any way I can, but you have to understand that some things are better left buried."

"Maybe," I admitted, my resolve unwavering. "But I can't keep running from my past. I need to face it head-on if I'm ever going to find peace."

Asa studied me for a long moment, his gaze inscrutable as he weighed his options.

"Alright," he finally agreed, his voice heavy with the

burden of secrets yet to be revealed. "If this is what you want, then I'll help you if I can."

"Thank you," I murmured, my heart swelling with gratitude and something akin to hope.

"Remember, though," Asa's eyes bore into mine, their intensity sending shivers down my spine, "once we start down this path, there's no turning back."

"I know," I replied, nodding resolutely. "But I'm ready."

If uncovering the truth meant navigating the wrath of the Irish mafia, then so be it. For the sake of my family and our shattered past, I would face whatever dangers lay ahead. I may have just made the worst mistake of my life. It was a risk I had to take, though. I'd either end up dead, or I'd get my answers, and the justice I wanted for my mom and my sister.

8

____

Robin

The windows inside the diner on the outskirts of New Orleans, somewhere called Metairie, were steamed up as rain pounded down outside. I didn't really notice that, or that my coffee was going or that my sandwich was equally as cold. My fingers traced the rim of my mug, my attention consumed by my thoughts, my memories of my mother and sister, their faces forever etched in my mind. I had vowed to seek justice for them, and as the daunting task before me became clear, my resolve wavered. Could I really get them justice? Could I do this on my own? And could Asa really help me or was he setting me up to end up just like Mom and Angela?

"Can I get you anything else?" the waitress asked, her voice pulling me from my reverie.

I shook my head, forcing a small smile. "No, thank you."

As she left, the bell above the door to the diner jingled, signaling another customer's arrival. An icy draft followed him in, chilling me to the bone. Detective James Harrison's tired eyes scanned the room, his gaze finally landing on me. Time seemed to slow as he approached, his footsteps deliberate and heavy. The detective's graying hair framed a weathered face that told a story of unrelenting determination. He carried an air of authority that demanded attention; it was a presence impossible to ignore.

My hope sprang to life as Detective Harrison approached my table, his footsteps echoing through the quiet diner like thunder on a stormy night. A shiver ran down my spine, and I tightened my grip on my coffee cup, as if holding onto it would steady me. The flickering light overhead cast eerie shadows across his face, adding to the sense of unease that settled in the pit of my stomach.

"Robin?" he asked, his voice low and gravelly. His dark eyes flickered over me, making observations his face didn't reveal. It was probably best that way. I didn't want to know what he sensed about me.

"Hi, yeah, that's me. Join me," I managed to say, anticipation making me nervous. Could this man help me? I'd hoped he could, when I finally dug out the card Angela had given to me and called him.

"Detective Jim Harrison," he introduced himself, extending a hand for me to shake. His grasp was firm, yet gentle, much like his demeanor. "I'm not sure how I can help you in your quest for justice, Robin, but I do want to help."

His tone was serious and determined, each word weighed down by an unspoken promise to uncover the truth. As my eyes met his, I saw a fire burning behind them, a fire that matched my own, born from pain and loss. It was clear that this was no mere whim; he was as committed to this cause as I was.

"Okay. Well, you're the detective that found my sister,

that got her home safely to us. What can you tell me about the man who took my sister?" My voice wavered, betraying my vulnerability.

"First, let's get out of here," he suggested, glancing at the empty tables around us. "Somewhere we can speak more freely."

"Alright," I agreed, the tension in my chest loosening ever so slightly. We stood up together, the scrape of our chairs against the wooden floor echoing through the room. As we walked toward the door, Detective Harrison's heavy footsteps seemed to reverberate within me, a constant reminder of the gravity of the situation.

"Where are we going?" I asked, my breath taken away by the sultry heat as we stepped outside.

"Somewhere safe. Trust me," he said, his voice steady but laced with the same melancholic tone that seemed to haunt us both.

As we walked side by side in silence, I couldn't help but feel a strange mix of comfort and unease wash over me. Detective Harrison's presence brought with it the promise of answers, yet also the weight of uncertainty. Would the truth bring me solace, or would it unleash even greater darkness?

"Robin," he spoke, as if reading my thoughts. "I know this is difficult for you, but I want you to know that I'm here to help you find justice, whatever it takes."

His words hung in the air, heavy with both hope and sorrow. And as we continued on into the night, I clung to that hope, praying that it would be enough to see me through the dark days that lay ahead. My heart pounded in my chest as I studied Detective Harrison's face, searching for any hint of deception. The dim light from the streetlamps outside cast shadows that seemed to deepen the lines on his face, making him appear both weary and resolute at the same time.

"Forgive me if I seem skeptical," I said, my voice barely above a whisper as I struggled to contain the storm of emotions brewing within me. "But why would you risk everything to help a complete stranger?"

Detective Harrison sighed deeply, his shoulders slumping as if weighed down by an invisible burden. "Because I failed her once before."

He paused, his gaze focused on some distant point beyond the window, and when he continued, his voice was heavy with regret. "I was the one who helped Angela escape from the man she knew as Ryan Hawkins. That's not his real name. It's Declan O'Sullivan. I'm just sorry I couldn't prove it before her death. I did everything I could to protect her, but in the end, it wasn't enough."

The weight of his guilt hit me like a tidal wave, threatening to swallow me whole. The pain in his eyes mirrored my own, and for a moment, our shared loss connected us in a way I couldn't quite understand. But as the reality of his words sunk in, my resolve hardened once more, and I forced myself to confront the truth head-on.

"You did everything you could for my sister. Why did you think you failed her? What else could you have done?" The questions tumbled out, each one laced with a mixture of hope and dread.

"Saving Angela wasn't enough," he admitted, his voice quivering ever so slightly. "She was desperate to get away from him and went back home before I could do anything about him. I tried to talk her out of leaving, but she couldn't be in this city, so close to him, anymore. I did everything in my power to get her to safety. But they found her again...and this time, there was nothing I could do."

As he spoke, I saw the pain and guilt etched across his features, and my own heart ached in sympathy. I knew all too well the torment of feeling responsible for a loved one's suffering, and it was a burden I wouldn't wish on anyone.

"Detective Harrison," I murmured, my voice barely audible against the low hum of the city outside. "You can't blame yourself for what happened to Angela. She made her own choices, just as we all do."

He looked at me then, his eyes brimming with an emotion I couldn't quite define. It was as if he saw something within me that both frightened and intrigued him, and despite my lingering reservations, I felt a strange sense of kinship with this man who had tried so desperately to save my sister.

"Robin," he began, his voice soft and full of compassion. "I know that you have every reason not to trust me. But I want you to understand that I'm on your side. And if you'll let me, I would like to help you find the answers you're searching for."

As I stared into Detective Harrison's eyes, I found myself torn between hope and fear, hope that the truth might finally be within my grasp, and fear that it could destroy me in the process. But as I weighed the risks and rewards, I realized that I would never find peace unless I confronted the shadows of my past, no matter how painful they might be. That's why I'd called him and asked him to meet me at the diner, wasn't it?

"Alright," I whispered, my voice trembling with uncertainty. "I'll trust you...for now."

I blinked back the tears that threatened to spill over as I considered Detective Harrison's offer of assistance. On the one hand, his knowledge and experience could prove invaluable in my quest for justice. But on the other hand, it meant relinquishing some control, trusting someone other than myself with the fate of my family.

"Robin," Detective Harrison said, breaking the silence between us. "You need to understand the world you're stepping into. The men in that organization, the man that runs it, it's not just a group of criminals. It's a web of lies and deceit. Relationships are built on manipulation, and loyalty can shift in an instant."

His words pierced through me like shards of ice, sending shivers down my spine. Asa's face bloomed in my mind, a dark portrait that made me shiver. As much as I wanted to believe that Asa was different, that he was somehow immune to the twisted machinations of the underworld, I knew that I couldn't afford to be naive. My sister and mother's deaths proved that.

"Okay," I breathed, coming to a decision. "What do you know about a man named Asa Kelly?"

"I know enough to tell you to stay away from him. And Declan." Jim's eyes bore into mine, heavy with worry. I nearly smiled at the fatherly look.

"How dangerous is he? What else can you tell me about him?" I asked, my voice barely audible.

"Only that you should be careful," he replied, his expression grave. "He may seem charming but remember that charm is often the best disguise. You're walking into dangerous territory, Robin. The closer you get to people like Asa Kelley, the more likely you are to find yourself caught in the crossfire."

As Detective Harrison's warning echoed in my mind, a knot of anxiety began to form in the pit of my stomach. I had suspected all along that pursuing a relationship with Asa might come at a cost, yet until now, I hadn't fully grasped just how high those stakes might be. Belinda had tried to warn me, but I'd ignored those warnings, blinded by his smile and my need to get out of my own head. But maybe I could use Asa to get to the man I wanted to get my hands on the most?

"Thank you," I murmured, my fingers in the pockets of my jeans. "I'll keep that in mind."

"Good," he said, nodding solemnly. "Just remember that if you ever need help, or even just someone to talk to, you can always reach out to me. I may not have been able to save your sister, but I'll do everything in my power to ensure that you don't meet the same fate."

I watched Detective Harrison's face closely, searching for any sign of deceit. But his eyes remained steady, and his voice never wavered as he began to share the secrets of a world I had only glimpsed from afar.

"What can you tell me about this Declan guy, then?" I asked, finding a park bench to sit on and sat down, not minding that my bottom got a little wet. Jim stood near me, watching the people hurrying by before he answered.

"Declan O'Sullivan rules the Irish mafia here with an iron fist," he began, taking a deep breath before continuing. "He has his fingers in nearly every criminal enterprise you can imagine: drug trafficking, illegal gambling, human smuggling...you name it."

As he spoke, images of Asa flashed through my mind: the way he moved with lethal grace, the dangerous glint in his gray eyes. Could the man I had become addicted to truly be part of such a brutal organization?

"His power is absolute within his ranks," Detective Harrison went on, "but that doesn't mean there aren't those who would challenge him. The Irish mafia is riddled with internal strife, factions vying for control. One wrong move could ignite a war."

I swallowed hard, feeling the weight of his words settle like lead in my stomach. If I accepted Detective Harrison's help, would I be able to navigate this treacherous underworld without losing myself, or worse, inadvertently causing harm to those I sought to protect?

"Even if you manage to avoid the crossfire," he continued, his tone somber, "there's still the matter of trust. Asa may seem genuine, and he might even care for you to some extent, but don't forget where his loyalties lie. In the end, blood will always run thicker than water."

"He's related to Declan?" I asked, my blood freezing cold.

"They're cousins." Detective Harrison revealed and I closed my eyes as my heart squeezed painfully.

The thought of betraying Asa tore at my heart, leaving me raw and exposed. But he was Declan's cousin? I knew that accepting Detective Harrison's advice would mean putting distance between us, perhaps irrevocably so. And yet, I couldn't ignore the nagging voice in the back of my mind that whispered: what if he's right?

"Take your time, Robin," Detective Harrison said softly, breaking through the storm of my thoughts. "I won't push you into a decision. Just know that if you ever need help, I'll be there."

I stared down at my trembling hands, the turmoil within me reflected in the ripples that danced across the surface of my untouched coffee. Was it worth it? Was seeking justice for my family worth the risk of losing everything? Could I trust Detective Harrison enough to let him guide me through the darkness that lay ahead?

Only one thing was certain: whatever path I chose, there would be no turning back. And as I sat there, alone and adrift, I knew that the decision before me would come to define not only my future but the very essence of who I was.

"Thanks, detective. You know where I'm staying. If you find out anything else, please let me know, okay? I'd like to get justice for my family and see that man Declan behind bars," I said, hoping he didn't hear the lie in my voice. I wanted Declan underground, not in prison.

"Will do," he said with a smile he put me in a cab and watched me leave. As Detective Harrison faded into the distance, I was left alone with my thoughts once more. The weight of his words hung heavy on my heart, casting a shadow over all that I had believed about Asa and the world he inhabited.

But even as the doubts and fears swirled within me, a stubborn flame of hope continued to burn, a hope that despite the darkness that surrounded us, there was still a chance to make some good out of the mess I was in. As I stared down at the detective's business card in the flashes of the streetlights, its edges now creased from my anxious fidgeting, I knew that only time would reveal whether that hope could withstand the storm that lay ahead.

As the door to my room closed behind, I felt a chill sweep over me, as though I had been abandoned to face an impending storm on my own. The world beyond the motel windows seemed distant and distorted, like a puzzle whose pieces no longer fit together. And somewhere within that fractured landscape, the truth I sought lay hidden, shrouded beneath layers of deception and betrayal.

My fingers tightened around Detective Harrison's business card, crumpling its edges. Could I trust him? The question circled endlessly through my mind, a relentless tide that threatened to pull me under. He had offered me a lifeline, but accepting it meant navigating uncharted waters, teeming with dangers I could scarcely imagine.

And what of Asa? My heart ached at the thought of

pushing him away, of trading the warmth of his embrace for the cold, unforgiving pursuit of justice. But if the darkness within him was as deep and impenetrable as Detective Harrison had suggested, could we ever really be anything meaningful?

I stared down at the card in my hand, its creased surface a testament to the turmoil that raged within me. The choice was mine, and mine alone. In that moment, I realized that my quest for justice had taken an unexpected turn, branching off into tangled paths whose destinations remained shrouded in uncertainty.

A heavy sigh escaped my lips as I gazed out at the rain-slicked streets, my eyes tracing the path of a solitary drop as it traced its way down the windowpane. Like me, it was caught between two worlds, suspended in a place where the lines between truth and deception blurred like ink in water.

As I clutched Detective Harrison's card to my pounding heart, I knew that whatever path I chose, there would be no turning back. And with each heartbeat that echoed through the empty room, the sense of foreboding that lingered in the air grew heavier, casting a shadow over all that lay ahead.

9

Robin

The dimly lit corner of the crowded Irish pub seemed to call my name the next day, a beacon in the midst of chaos. My heart raced as I navigated the room, each step feeling heavier than the last. The warmth of sunshine barely made it through the windows behind me, casting shadows on the worn wooden walls adorned with fading pictures and memorabilia. The scent of stale beer and smoke clung to the air as laughter and voices intermingled like a symphony of secrets.

As if pulled by an invisible thread, my gaze locked onto Asa's piercing gray eyes. The intensity of his stare felt like a lifeline in this sea of uncertainty. We exchanged subtle glances and secret smiles as we drew closer, the magnetic pull between us undeniable.

"Robin," he whispered softly, his voice like silk against my ears. His muscular frame towered over me, creating a sense of security that I hadn't realized I'd been craving.

"Hi, Asa," I replied, my voice registering amidst the cacophony surrounding us. We carefully chose our words, speaking in hushed tones to avoid drawing attention from anyone that might overhear us. Our conversation was a delicate dance, each word weighed down by the gravity of our situation.

"Let's get a drink, shall we?" Asa suggested, his disarming smile causing my heart to skip a beat. I nodded, reveling in the fleeting moments of normalcy as we made our way to the bar. The clink of glasses and the murmur of subdued conversations created a tapestry of sound that enveloped us.

"Guinness for me, and..." Asa trailed off, his eyes searching mine for an answer. I let out a small laugh, grateful for the opportunity to escape into the familiarity of our connection.

"Jameson, please," I answered, my brown eyes meeting his once more. The bartender nodded and set to work, expertly pouring our drinks with practiced ease.

As we sipped our respective beverages, the weight of our circumstances pressed down upon us. The room felt smaller, more suffocating, as if the walls were closing in around us. My mind wandered to the ghosts of my past, their memories haunting me like a phantom embrace.

"Robin," Asa murmured, his hand brushing against mine beneath the bar. The warmth of his touch sent shivers down my spine, a stark contrast to the icy grip of fear that had taken hold of my heart. "We'll figure this out, together."

His words hung in the air like a promise, one I desperately wanted to believe. But as I stared into the depths of his gray eyes, I couldn't help but wonder if what we had could last, or if our connection would only serve to deepen the shadows that threatened to consume us both. He pulled at my hand, guiding me to a table, distracting me.

In the dimly lit corner of the crowded pub, I could feel the weight of countless eyes upon us. Whispers and murmurs filled the air like fog, a shroud of suspicion that clung to my every breath. I caught glimpses of stern faces and raised eyebrows from some of the other people in the bar as they took notice of our secretive exchange. The growing curiosity surrounding my connection to Asa was palpable, a heavy stone in the pit of my stomach.

Why had he asked me to meet him here, if his associated would be here too? Was I in danger?

"Everything alright?" Asa asked quietly, his eyes searching my face for any sign of distress.

"Y-yes," I stammered, struggling to maintain my composure. "I just...I can feel their eyes on us."

Asa's gaze swept across the room, assessing the situation with practiced precision. Without a word, he subtly shifted his body to shield me from prying eyes, his presence creating a protective barrier around me. It was a small gesture, but one that spoke volumes about his loyalty and devotion.

"Let them look," he said softly, his voice steady and reassuring. "We have nothing to hide, Robin. We're just lovers, having a drink together, right?"

As much as I wanted to believe him, a nagging doubt lingered at the edge of my thoughts. In this world of shadows and secrets, could I truly withstand the scrutiny of those who sought to tear me apart, or would, if they found out exactly who I was? The answer eluded me, slipping through my fingers like smoke.

"Everything is so uncertain, Asa," I whispered, my heart aching with the weight of unspoken fears. "How do we navigate this dangerous game without losing ourselves?"

"By staying true to who we are, and never letting go of what we hold dear," he replied, his conviction unwavering. "Trust me, Robin. I'm here for you. We're having drinks, then we'll go to dinner or something. Nothing more, nothing less, so stay calm, alright?"

I couldn't, though, not when it made no sense as to why he'd asked me to come here.

"Why did you ask me here, Asa," I whispered to him, leaning in closer so our eyes met.

"Because if I stay away too long, people will come looking for me. People you don't want anything to do with." His words were cryptic and sent a chill down my spine. "But I'll protect you. I promise."

His words wrapped themselves around my heart like a warm embrace, but the cold tendrils of doubt refused to release their grasp. As we sat there, entwined in our own private world, I knew that our journey was far from over. I felt a flicker of hope, a tiny flame that burned amidst the shadows, promising the possibility of escape and the sweet taste of freedom. But was it only my imagination?

Nestled in that shadowy corner, surrounded by the enigmatic figures that instinctively noted our every move, I clung to Asa's whispered words. In a world where trust was currency and betrayal an ever-present threat, it was all we had to hold on to. And perhaps, it was enough.

The air around us seemed to thicken, a heavy fog of suspicion that clung to our skin. The quiet murmurs and clinking glasses that filled the crowded pub were a stark contrast to the storm brewing within me. Asa's warm breath tickled my ear, his voice a low hum as he whispered sweet words of reassurance to me as the night carried on.

"Trust me, Robin," he said, the soft brush of his lips against my skin sending shivers down my spine. I glanced up at him, my brown eyes meeting his gray ones, searching for any hint of doubt or hesitation. But all I found was unwavering resolve, a fierce determination that made my heart race with equal parts fear and desire.

In response, I reached out tentatively, my fingertips grazing the rough skin of his hand. Our covert touches, bold yet fleeting, served as an anchor amidst the turbulent sea of uncertainty that surrounded us. With each stolen kiss, each gentle caress, we forged an unspoken bond, a silent promise that we would weather this storm together, whatever the cost.

As we moved through the room, our bodies pressed close in a dance of deception and desire, Asa effortlessly engaged in conversations with other mafia members, his charm and wit a perfect shield to deflect attention from our growing connection. I admired his skill, the ease with which he navigated these dangerous waters, but I couldn't help but feel a pang of unease, a nagging doubt that gnawed at the edges of my mind.

"*Can I truly trust him?*" I wondered, my thoughts a tangled web of fear and longing. "*Is his loyalty to me stronger than his ties to these people?*"

The weight of these questions bore down on me, a suffocating pressure that threatened to crush the fragile hope that bloomed within my heart. And yet, as I looked into Asa's eyes, saw the fierce protectiveness that lurked within their depths, I couldn't help but believe in the possibility of redemption, of finding a way out of this twisted maze of lies and deceit.

"Robin," Asa murmured, his voice quiet in the din of the

pub. "I know this isn't easy, but we only need to stay a little while longer."

His words were like a balm to my frayed nerves, a soothing caress that eased the tight knot of fear coiled within my chest. I nodded, swallowing hard as I fought to keep my emotions in check.

"Alright," I whispered, my voice wavering with the effort to remain calm. "I can do this, Asa."

I could feel the tension build like a crescendo, the notes of unease reverberating through the air. My heart raced as I caught my first glimpse of Declan O'Sullivan, his salt-and-pepper hair and sharp jawline unmistakable even in the dimly lit pub. I'd found pictures of him in old newspapers so he was much older now, but that was him. His penetrating gaze was like a scalpel cutting through the layers of my psyche, the unreadable mix of curiosity and suspicion making me shiver involuntarily.

He had to know who I was, surely? Or did he have so many women kidnapped and killed that my sister's face was just a vague memory that he couldn't recall? At that moment, I hoped it was. Declan O'Sullivan oozed evil and it made my skin crawl.

"Robin," Asa whispered into my ear, his breath warm against my skin, "stay close to me."

As if I'd step away from him with a monster like that in the room with me. That man was responsible for some seriously heinous crimes and for the death of my sister and mother. I didn't want to be anywhere near him. Still, I nodded, aware of every inch of space between us as we navigated the crowded room together.

"Ah, Mr. Kelley," a voice called out, thick with a lilting Irish accent. "A pleasure to see you here tonight."

"Likewise, Liam," Asa replied, effortlessly shifting gears as he engaged in conversation with one of Declan's associates. His charm and charisma seemed to work like magic, drawing people in and putting them at ease. Yet, I noticed how Asa subtly maintained his protective stance around me, his muscular frame acting as a barrier between myself and the prying eyes of the Irish mafia members.

"I think I'm a little jealous, Asa," Liam murmured, sipping from his glass, "who is this enchanting lady you've brought with you?"

My pulse quickened, realizing the delicate balance Asa needed to maintain in order to keep me out of harm's way. He still didn't know my entire story, but he knew I was here to find a man like Declan, maybe even suspected it was Declan himself, but he hadn't pushed for answers. I held my breath as he answered with a disarming smile.

"Robin is an old friend of mine," he said smoothly. "She's been away for some time but has recently returned to New Orleans. I thought it would be nice to introduce her to our...mutual acquaintances."

"Indeed," Liam replied, eyeing me with interest. "Well, welcome back to the city, Robin. I hope you find your stay...enlightening."

"Thank you," I managed, forcing a polite smile as my mind raced with apprehension.

As Asa continued to navigate the treacherous waters of mafia politics, skimming the surface of conversations while expertly avoiding any hidden depths, I couldn't help but feel both admiration and fear for this man who had become so entwined with my heart. Could we escape the suffocating grasp of this dark world we found ourselves in? Or were we doomed to be swallowed by the shadows that lurked in every corner?

"Robin," Asa murmured as we moved through the room, "remember what I told you earlier. I'll take care of you. Stay calm."

My fingers brushed against his as we exchanged fleeting touches, our connection a lifeline amidst the swirling vortex of danger that surrounded us. And as my eyes met Asa's once more, I clung to the hope that together, we might just be able to outrun the darkness. The clink of glasses and the low hum of conversation surrounded us, but my senses felt heightened, attuned to every dangerous undercurrent that pulsed through the room. A whispered threat here, a veiled warning there, it was as if the very air we breathed carried the weight of secrets and lies.

"Robin," Asa said softly, leaning in so close that his warm breath fanned over my ear, "I can tell you're uneasy. Please, relax."

"Thank you," I whispered back, feeling his strong arm brush against mine as he subtly maneuvered me away from prying ears. My heart pounded in my chest as I searched the dimly lit space for hidden dangers, for eyes that lingered just a moment too long on our forms.

As the night wore on, I noticed that we were becoming increasingly isolated. Our interactions with other mafia members grew more guarded, more cautious. Each wary glance and curt nod threatened to betray our secret alliance, and I could feel the invisible walls closing in around us.

"Are you alright?" Asa asked, his gray eyes searching my face for any sign of distress.

"I'm okay," I lied, the words tasting like ash on my tongue. Inside, a storm of doubt and fear raged, threatening to consume me. How could I reconcile the things I felt for this man with the suspicions that gnawed at the edges of my mind? Was our connection strong enough to withstand the crushing pressure of the world he inhabited?

"Let's get some fresh air," Asa suggested, sensing my growing agitation. He guided me toward the exit, his hand resting protectively on the small of my back as we slipped out into the cool night.

Outside, the tension that had been coiling within me began to dissipate, replaced by a fragile sense of relief. In that quiet moment, away from the oppressive atmosphere of the pub, I allowed myself to sink into Asa's embrace, my body trembling with a mixture of fear and desire.

"It's okay, Robin," he murmured against my hair, "I'm right here."

"Asa," a voice called out of the darkness, rough and thick with an accent I didn't quite recognize. "Come here."

Beneath the dim glow of flickering streetlights, I studied Asa's face as he spoke to one of his associates, his eyes narrowed with a steely intensity that sent shivers down my spine. The conversation felt as if it stretched on for an eternity, and I struggled to maintain my composure as my heart threatened to tear itself from my chest.

Asa cut off the other man's words with a charming smile and said something that seemed to relieve the guy. He nodded at the man then came back to me, his face hard until he caught my eyes. He took my hand in his, leading me to an alcove hidden behind a worn wooden pillar. In that shadowy corner, we were safe from prying eyes, at least for a moment.

Asa's lips found mine in a feverish kiss, his hands tangling in my hair with a desperation that mirrored my own. In those stolen moments, our connection felt like a lifeline, a tether to sanity that I quickly felt like I was losing.

"Robin," Asa whispered between kisses, "I know your mind is racing with questions and doubts. Tonight must have been a real eye-opener, but I've got you."

I stared up at him, wondering about his need to constantly reassure me. What was that about? And did he really think he could protect me from a man like Declan?

"Can you really promise me that?" I asked breathlessly, feeling the weight of my fears bearing down on my shoulders. "Can you truly keep me safe from this world?"

"I'll do everything within my power," he vowed, his gaze filled with a fierce determination that both comforted and frightened me.

We stood there, pressed together in the shadows, seeking solace in each other's touch as the murmur of conversations and clinking glasses from inside the pub filled the air around us. With every stolen caress, my resolve weakened and my need for Asa deepened, leaving me teetering on the edge of surrender. But even as I allowed myself to indulge in these fleeting moments of intimacy, I couldn't silence the nagging voice in the back of my mind, whispering warnings of the consequences our relationship might bring. What future could we possibly have in this world of deception and danger? Would I be strong enough to weather the storms that loomed on the horizon?

"Robin," Asa murmured, his fingers tracing the curve of my cheek as if he could read the turmoil in my thoughts, "I promise."

His words were soothed my fractured heart, but they couldn't banish the shadows of doubt that lingered at the edge of my consciousness. As our stolen moments came to an end, we reluctantly pulled away from one another, steeling ourselves for the battles yet to come. With each step back into the pub, I felt the suffocating weight of uncertainty and unease pressing down upon me once more, a constant reminder of the dangerous path we had chosen. But through it all, Asa's hand remained steadfastly entwined with mine.

I could feel the air thicken around us as we retreated to a secluded corner of the pub, Asa's arm encircling my waist like an anchor in the storm. The dimly lit room seemed to close in around us, its shadows heavy with unspoken secrets and whispered threats. Yet, in that cocoon of darkness, I found solace in the heat of his body pressed against mine, a beacon of light amidst the chaos.

"Are you alright?" Asa asked softly, concern etching itself into the lines of his face as he gazed down at me, his gray eyes seeking out the truth hidden beneath my carefully constructed mask of indifference.

I forced a smile, trying to keep the tremors of fear from betraying my resolve. "I'm fine."

His fingers brushed against my cheek, tender and hesitant, as if he might shatter the fragile illusion I clung to so desperately.

"You don't have to pretend with me, Robin," he whispered, his breath warm against my skin, "I know how hard this is for you."

My heart clenched at his admission, the weight of my emotions threatening to crush the feeble barriers that held them at bay. Did he really know, though? How could he?

"Can we go soon?" I asked, my voice wavering, "It's so oppressive in here. I'm not sure how much more I can take."

"Of course, just a little while longer," he pulled me closer, the strength of his embrace offering a sense of security I hadn't known I craved. As I listened to the steady thrum of his heartbeat, I allowed myself to be enveloped by the warmth of his conviction, letting it chase away the shadows of doubt that had taken root in my soul.

His lips brushed ever so faintly against mine, a gentle reminder of the strange bond we shared. All I could do was stand at his side, watching gangsters, likely murderers, drug dealers, and human traffickers hobnobbing with each other. I needed a drink, but right now? I wasn't going to accept a drink from anyone, not even Asa. I'd have one back in my room later. Where it was safe.

10

———————

Asa

The cool night air bit at my skin as we left the dimly lit backroom of the gathering, Robin's hand in mine, her pulse a frantic rhythm against my fingers. Her wide brown eyes had mirrored my own fury, her fear so palpable it felt like another entity in the room, a shadow haunting us both.

"Let's get you out of here," I murmured, more to myself than to her. The choked nod she gave me was all the confirmation I needed to whisk her away from Declan and his band of cutthroats who masqueraded as businessmen.

Once we were inside my car, the roar of the engine drowned out the chaos of the city, offering a fleeting sanctuary. But the silence between us was a stark reminder that no matter how fast I drove, I couldn't outrun the life I'd been trying to leave behind for years. Declan's grip on my world was tenacious, his influence seeping into every crack and crevice, even as I fought to pry myself free from his hold.

By the time we reached my place, the tension within me

had coalesced into something primal, an urgency that demanded release. As the front door closed behind us, I pressed Robin against it, my hands roaming over her with a possessiveness that bordered on desperation. I needed to feel her, to remind myself that there was still warmth and humanity left in me, despite the coldness of the life I led.

"Sorry," I half-growled, pulling her dress up, not waiting for permission as I tore her panties away. A sharp inhale from her lips told me she wasn't opposed, but rather anticipating what came next. This need between us was a living thing, always clawing its way to the surface whenever we were near each other.

I could feel the ghost of Declan lingering in the corners of my mind, reminding me of the man I could never truly escape. Every moment spent distancing myself from him felt like I was swimming against an insurmountable current. And yet, there was Robin, the one answer I could give her without reservation, the honesty of my body against hers.

"Are you okay?" I asked, my voice barely more than a rasp. Her nod and the slight parting of her lips were all the encouragement I needed. Cupping her face, I bent down, taking her nipple into my mouth, savoring the soft gasp that escaped her as I did. There was a raw purity in this act, one that eclipsed every doubt and every fear.

Burying my face in the crook of her neck, I took a moment to breathe her in, the scent of her skin mingling with the faint traces of danger and smoke that seemed to follow me wherever I went. It was in these quiet moments, with her beneath my touch, that the possibility of something real flickered to life, stubborn and unyielding.

I turned her body, not certain if I just wanted to press myself into her ass or if I didn't want her to see me, to... judge me. The door finally clicked shut as she leaned against it, the sound echoing through the empty space like a start pistol, and I was off. My hands were rough as they roamed over her, an urgency driving my every movement. I could feel the tension in her body, the way she braced against the door as if preparing for a storm.

"Do you want it in your ass tonight, or do you want my cock in your pussy, hard and brutal, fucking you until you scream for me to stop?" I growled into her ear, my breath hot on her skin. "But I'm not going to stop, not tonight, sweetheart. I'm going to fuck you until I have my fill."

She shuddered, a small whimper betraying her desires. She craved the hardness, the relentless pounding of flesh on flesh that left us both gasping and spent. Tonight, there would be no tenderness, just the raw need that simmered between us.

I stripped away my clothes without finesse, yanking at the fabric that clung to my body. When I went back to her, my fingers found her nipples, squeezing until she squirmed, making pained noises that only spurred me on. Her breasts filled my hands, firm and demanding attention.

"Or do you want to just suck my dick until I come down your throat, baby?" My voice was heavy, thick with lust as I pressed closer, harder between her ass, pinning her with my hips. "Tell me, Robin? What do you want tonight?"

Her answer was a moan, wordless and laden with desire. It was all the confirmation I needed. Every fiber of my being strained toward her, needing to claim, to possess. I had started this dangerous game with the intent to merely play, but somewhere along the line, the stakes had changed. Now, it wasn't just about satisfaction, it was about chasing away the demons.

As our bodies collided, there was no room for doubts, no space for the shadows that hunted me. There was only

Robin and the sweet escape she offered, a temporary reprieve from a world that demanded too much and forgave too little. And as I lost myself in her, I couldn't help but wonder how long this illusion of safety could last.

Then she claimed my attention again with her whimpered words. "I just want you, however you want me, Asa."

Those words unraveled the last threads of my restraint. I was a man teetering on the edge of control, yet her submission, her absolute trust in me, anchored me enough to remember the rules of the game we played. It wasn't about taking, it was about giving. And tonight, I was going to give until she was undone, a soft, satiated mess beneath my touch.

The cool air of the living room contrasted with the heat of our entwined bodies as I nudged her toward the couch. Her nakedness was a testament to the urgency that had consumed us both from the moment we left Declan's poisonous presence. Every curve and dip of her flesh begged for attention, and I was a willing devotee at the altar of her pleasure.

In one fluid motion, I leaned her over the back of the couch, the position leaving her exposed, open to me in every way that mattered. My middle finger found the tight ring of her ass, pressing in as my tongue delved into the slick heat of her pussy. She squirmed against my face, not trying to escape but seeking more, pushing back to meet each flick, each suckle of my mouth. Her hands clutched at the cushions, her body a beautiful canvas of need.

"Take it, baby, take my finger deep inside you," I growled, my voice thick with the same need that had filled her. Her pussy clenched around my finger, sparking a jolt of pleasure that washed over me as I worked my thick middle finger deeper into her ass.

"You want it like this, don't you?" I asked, not waiting for her answer. "You want me to take you like this, hard and dirty?"

My finger twisted inside her, an aggressive motion that was matched by the violent thrust of my tongue against her. I knew the pain that I inflicted would only be a catalyst for her pleasure, but I wasn't here to alleviate that pain. I was here to make her feel everything she had ever wanted.

"Fuck, Asa," she gasped, her voice muffled by the cushions. "It's too much."

But it wasn't enough. I needed to hear her beg for it, to beg for her release.

"Oh, baby, it's just the beginning, just wait until I slide my cock into that sweet pussy of yours," I growled, the dirty words spurring her on.

Her free hand clawed at the fabric of the couch, her nails digging into the material for support. Her hips undulated with the rhythm of my finger, her pussy dripping with her arousal. I could hear the slippery sound of my tongue in her pussy and the way she panted, in between the moans she couldn't stop.

With my free hand, I reached between her thighs, stroking my fingers through her glistening folds. She was more than ready for me, and I was more than ready to take her. But not yet.

"I'm going to fuck you so hard, baby, so hard that you'll scream my name," I murmured, my breath hot and heavy against her skin.

She shuddered beneath me, her body trembling with her pleasure.

"More, Asa...please," she gasped between breaths, and I could feel her muscles tensing, coiling tight like a spring ready to snap. Hearing her beg, feeling her body writhe under the ministrations of my fingers and tongue, it was almost too much. Almost.

But I held on, because this was about her unraveling, her release. That was what made it worth it, the sight, the sound, the taste of Robin losing herself completely. And when she did, when she came apart under my hands, I knew that despite all the shadows that dogged my heels, there was light in this world. For now, at least.

I watched her, every quiver and shudder under my touch a silent conversation between us. Her body spoke in trembles and gasps, telling me all I needed to know. She didn't have to say anything, her desires were laid bare before me, as naked and raw as her skin against the coolness of the couch.

Her need for control, or rather, her desire to relinquish it tonight, was clear. In the dim light of the living room, with shadows dancing on the walls from the flickering candles I'd lit earlier, I felt the weight of her trust pressing down on me, heavier than any physical force. It was my responsibility, my privilege, to be the one she surrendered to, and I took that role with a gravity that matched the intensity of our connection.

And damn, did I love her for it. The words had been bubbling under the surface for god knows how long, but I'd never let them out. Maybe I was scared they'd be another casualty in our world of fractured loyalties and broken promises. Robin and I, we were both damaged goods, too familiar with betrayal to ever truly let our guards down. But here, in this moment, nothing else mattered.

As her pleasure built, rising like a crescendo that filled the space around us, she groaned, her voice hitting a pitch that vibrated straight to my core. And then, as if her body couldn't contain the sensation, it softened into a prolonged hum of ecstasy. That sound, it was pure music, a melody that resonated with the deepest parts of me.

"I think I love you, you crazy woman," I found myself saying, my voice barely above a whisper, rough with the emotion I struggled to keep in check. "I know I shouldn't say it, but I keep hoping, at some point, we'll heal each other, mend our hearts together." I paused, swallowing hard against the lump forming in my throat. "I don't know if it's real or not, love, but I think it is when I'm with you."

There was danger in those words, an uncertainty that twisted in my gut like a knife. But it was out there now, hanging between us, a confession that felt like stepping out into a void, not knowing if there was ground beneath my feet. With Robin, though, maybe I didn't mind falling.

As my whispered confession hung heavy in the air, her slender fingers wrapped around mine, guiding my hand to rest over the quickened beat of her heart. The tremors that had wracked her moments ago subsided into gentle after-shocks that still echoed through her frame. As I slid into her from behind, Robin's breath hitched, a soft gasp slipping from her lips that seemed to steal the very air from the room.

The heat of her surrounded me, the slick embrace of her body a testament to the raw desire we shared.

"I love how hot and wet you always are for me, Robin," I murmured against her ear, the words tumbling out laced with need. Her response was not in words but in the way she pushed back against me, urging me deeper, her movements saying more than any promise could.

"Fuck, I've never had a woman like you and I never want another after you." The truth of it weighed on my tongue, heavy and undeniable. Each thrust was a silent vow, an anchor in the chaos of our intertwined lives. "I just want to fuck you for the rest of my days."

And there it was, the unvarnished truth laid bare between us, as frightening as it was exhilarating.

Each motion blurred the lines between pleasure and something far more dangerous, something like hope. I sought solace in the rhythm we created, in the familiarity of her body yielding to mine. For those fleeting moments, I could almost forget the shadows that loomed outside the confines of this room, the threats that were never too far from our doorsteps.

The sense of escape was intoxicating, the illusion of safety within her arms a siren's call I couldn't resist. But then, reality would claw its way back, whispering warnings of the mystery and danger that threaded through our existence, reminding me that nothing was ever certain in our world, except perhaps this, the undeniable connection that kept pulling us back to each other.

Her body moved against mine with a rhythm that felt like the pulse of the night itself, each sway of her hips an echo of my own heartbeats. Robin's voice was low and husky, laden with desire as she twisted her neck to lock eyes with me. "I'm glad to hear that because I don't want to fuck anyone but you, Asa. You've got such a wonderful cock. Fill me with it, Asa. Fill me up until there's nothing left but you."

God, the way she talked, raw and unfiltered, it sent a surge of heat straight to my core, stoking the fire that raged within me. She was all heat and hunger, and her words wrapped around me, urging me to claim her even more fiercely.

I held back, though, drawing out the moment. The world outside faded away, it was just Robin and me, locked in our private dance of need and release. I watched her fingers drift down, teasing her swollen clit, pinching her nipples into hardened peaks. Her breaths came out in desperate gasps, and her body started to tremble with the rising tide of her orgasm.

That was when I gave in to the urgency that gnawed at me, thrusting harder into her as she crumbled beneath the onslaught of pleasure. A guttural growl tore from my throat as I joined her, our cries mingling in the charged air. This... this was what kept me tethered in a life where loyalties were as fickle as smoke, where every affection could be a prelude to betrayal.

In those moments, lost in the depths of her, the restlessness that always lurked in my bones quieted. The danger, the endless games of power, it all disappeared, leaving only the stark intensity of us. I could do this forever, drown in her over and over, if fate would only let me.

But wishing for forever was a dangerous game. In our world, forever was often cut short, and I knew that better than most. Yet as I held Robin close, feeling her heartbeat against my skin, I couldn't help but hope for just a little longer, a chance to live in the illusion that we were nothing but two lovers seeking solace in each other's arms.

11

———————

Robin

The damp cobblestones glistened beneath my feet as Asa and I made our way to the bar near my motel a few weeks later, a place where we could be more comfortable, away from those serpentine eyes of Declan O'Sullivan. Eyes that seemed far too interested in me.

As we entered, the bar's rich aroma of chicory coffee enveloped us like a warm embrace. A sultry jazz melody played in the background, mingling with the low hum of hushed conversations. The dimly lit interior cast an air of mystery over the patrons, their faces half-hidden in shadow. This was a place I could relax in, a place I could have that drink I'd wanted earlier.

"Over here," Belinda called softly, her delicate features illuminated by the flickering candlelight on the table. We slid into the booth across from her, our eyes meeting for the first time. Her innocent appearance belied the dangerous knowledge she carried, and my heart raced with anticipation.

"Thanks for meeting with us," Asa began, his smooth voice betraying none of the tension I felt. "We need your help."

"What'll it be?" Belinda asked, her brown eyes filled with curiosity.

"Scotch, please," I said quietly then looked at Asa. He asked for a beer and then we moved to a table with our drinks.

Belinda came over and sat down with us.

"I'll do whatever I can." She glanced around nervously before leaning in closer, her voice barely above a whisper. "Declan's been making some big moves lately, and people are starting to talk."

"What kind of moves?" I asked, my palms growing clammy against the cool surface of the table.

"Expanding his operations," she revealed, her eyes darting between Asa and me. "He's been meeting with some powerful people, even outside of the family operations I hear he's talking with some men from New York, up Robin's way. I think he's looking to strengthen his position in the city."

"Any idea why?" Asa pressed.

"Rumors say he's planning something big, something that would put him in control of more than just the gangs around here," she paused, her gaze dropping to the table. "I don't know exactly what it is, but I do know that it's making people nervous. They come in here, whispering about it a lot."

"Belinda, we need to find a way to bring him down," I said, my voice thick with desperation. Asa had finally convinced me to confide in Belinda, to accept the help she'd offered when I first arrived but had been too afraid to accept. "He took everything from me, my sister and my mother. I can't let him get away with it."

"I understand, Robin," she replied, her expression softening as she reached across the table to squeeze my hand. "I'll help you in any way I can."

"Thank you," I whispered, my eyes filling with unshed tears.

"First, we need to gather more information," Asa interjected, his gray eyes filled with resolve. "We need to know who Declan's new associates are and what he's planning."

"You should know all of that already, Asa. But leave that to me, I'll find out if you don't know," Belinda assured us, a determined glint in her eyes. "I'll keep my ears open at the bar. People tend to talk when they've had a few too many."

"Be careful, Belinda," Asa warned, concern etched on his face. "We don't want you getting caught up in this."

"I can handle myself," she said with a small smile, her confidence shining through. "You two focus on finding a way to stop Declan. If we work together, we can put an end to his reign of terror once and for all."

Asa nodded, his strong jaw set with determination. I couldn't help but steal glances at Belinda as we continued discussing our plan to put a stop Declan's operations. She had been an invaluable source of information, her innocent appearance belying the depth of her knowledge about Declan.

"Robin, are you sure you're ready for this?" Asa asked, his eyes filled with concern. "This is a dangerous game we're playing."

"I have to be," I replied, my voice barely above a whisper. "For Mom. For my sister. For all those who've suffered at Declan's hands."

As I spoke, I noticed a flicker of unease in Belinda's eyes. It was subtle, but unmistakable, a hint of vulnerability that made me wonder what secrets she might be hiding. Were there skeletons in her closet, too? Was she as much a victim of Declan's machinations as the rest of us?

"Belinda," I said gently, reaching out to touch her arm. "Are you alright?"

She hesitated for a moment before giving me a small, tight smile.

"I'm fine," she insisted, though the haunted look in her eyes told me otherwise. "Just worried about what we're getting ourselves into."

"Speaking of which...," Asa trailed off, his gaze shifting towards the entrance of the bar.

I followed his gaze and spotted Jim Harrison, his graying hair and tired eyes reflecting the weight of his years in law enforcement. He scanned the room, and upon seeing us, made his way over to our table.

"Detective Harrison," Asa greeted him cautiously, sliding over to make room for him. "What brings you here?"

"Call me Jim," he replied, his voice weary but firm. "I've been keeping tabs on Declan's activities, and I believe our interests align. I want to help bring him down."

"Are you sure we can trust him?" I asked Asa in a hushed tone, my heart pounding in my chest. I'd met with the man before, been comforted by him, but I'd learned early in life, trusting people can be dangerous. I wasn't even sure I could trust Asa, but I was trying to.

Asa hesitated, studying Jim's face for a long moment before finally nodding.

"Jim's the one who helped Angela escape New Orleans," he whispered back. "If it weren't for him, she wouldn't have made it as far as she did."

"Then we're all in this together," I said, meeting Jim's gaze. "We'll do whatever it takes to see justice done."

"Indeed," Jim agreed, a grim smile playing at the corners of his mouth. "It won't be easy, but with the right strategy, we might just stand a chance."

I properly introduced Jim to Belinda and told him how she could help gather information that we might need. They shook hands and then we got back down to business.

"Alright then," Asa said, clapping his hands together and looking around the table. "Let's get to work."

"Good," Jim began, his voice low and measured. "First things first, we need to ensure our activities don't draw any suspicion from either the Irish mafia or the police."

"Agreed," Asa chimed in, his eyes flickering with determination. "We'll have to be cautious and precise in our movements."

I felt my palms growing clammy beneath the table as I considered the immense weight of the task before us. My mind raced with thoughts of my family, the haunting memories that drove me to seek justice, no matter the cost.

"I can use my skills as a researcher to dig deeper into Declan's operations," I offered, trying to steady my voice. "It might help us uncover some valuable information without alerting anyone to our plans."

Asa nodded, placing a comforting hand on mine. His touch sent a surge of warmth through my body, a welcome reminder that I wasn't alone in this fight.

"That's a good idea, Robin," he said softly. "I can offer my knowledge of Declan's inner workings. I know how they operate and who we should be keeping an eye on."

"Excellent," Jim replied, his tired eyes betraying a hint of relief at our combined expertise. "Belinda, you're our eyes and ears within the organization. You'll need to continue playing the part of the innocent bystander while gathering intel for us."

Belinda's gaze wavered for a moment, her delicate features reflecting a flash of vulnerability I hadn't noticed before.

"I'll do my best," she whispered, her voice strained with a quiet resolve I couldn't help but admire. She might look fragile, innocent, maybe even vulnerable, but I'd learned a lot about her over the last few weeks. She was smart, strong, capable. She would do exactly what she'd promised.

"Remember," Jim cautioned, his words heavy with the weight of our shared burden. "One misstep could cost us everything."

We all nodded in agreement, acutely aware of the stakes that hung in the balance. With each passing moment, the shadows of the bar seemed to grow darker, as if reflecting the uncertainty and unease that simmered beneath the surface of our little group. It was a game of cat and mouse, and we were treading on dangerous ground.

"Let's get started then," Asa said, breaking the silence that had settled over us like a suffocating fog. "The sooner we uncover the truth behind Declan's connection to Rose and Angela's deaths, the sooner we can put an end to this nightmare."

"Absolutely," I murmured, my heart aching with longing for the closure we so desperately sought. "We owe it to them, and ourselves, to see this through to the end."

In that moment, with the taste of vengeance lingering on my tongue and the promise of retribution burning in my chest, I knew that nothing would stand in our way. We would fight tooth and nail, against the whispers of doubt and the looming specter of danger, to bring justice to those who had been wronged.

And with every beat of my heart, I swore to myself that we would not fail.

The sun dipped below the horizon, casting a veil of twilight over the city as we prepared to put our plan into action. The soft hum of conversation and clinking glassware around us felt like a distant echo, our focus sharpened by the task at hand. I glanced at Asa, his gray eyes reflecting the flickering candlelight that danced upon the table.

"Alright," he murmured, his voice low and controlled. "We've got our roles to play. Robin, you and I will work on infiltrating the mafia's social circles. That charity event tonight is the perfect opportunity for us to get close without raising any suspicions."

"Meanwhile, Belinda and I will gather information from our contacts," Jim added, his gruff voice tinged with determination. "We'll keep our ears open and report back anything we find."

"Sounds like a solid plan," I said, my fingers drumming rhythmically against the tabletop. "Let's hope it's enough to bring Declan and his operation down."

"Have faith, Robin," Belinda whispered, her brown eyes filled with quiet resolve. "We'll make sure justice is served."

Asa and I left the café, our steps echoing through the cobblestone streets of the French Quarter as we made our way to the exclusive charity event. The air was thick with the scent of magnolia blossoms and the promise of a sultry night. We walked in silence, the weight of our mission settling heavily upon us like an oppressive shroud.

Arriving at the grand mansion where the event was being held, we were greeted by the sight of opulence and decadence. Underneath the glittering chandeliers, men and women in their finest attire mingled, laughter and music filling the air. It was a world of illusion and deception, a fitting stage for our clandestine performance.

"Stay close and watch your back," Asa whispered into my ear as we entered the crowded ballroom, his warm breath sending shivers down my spine. I nodded, my heart racing in anticipation.

We moved through the crowd, our eyes scanning the sea of faces for any sign of Declan and his associates. It felt like walking a tightrope, each step carefully measured and balanced against the ever-present threat of discovery.

"Over there," Asa murmured, nodding subtly toward a group of men gathered near the bar. "There's Declan."

My breath caught in my throat as I studied the man who held the key to our vengeance. His salt-and-pepper hair and sharp jawline gave him an air of authority and power, his confident stance a testament to the influence he wielded over those around him.

"Stay close to me," Asa instructed, leading me toward the group. Our approach was casual, calculated, as if we were merely two guests drawn by idle curiosity. We listened intently, straining to pick up any valuable information from their conversation.

"Declan mentioned something about a shipment," I whispered to Asa as we drifted away from the group, my pulse quickening with excitement. "It sounded important."

"Let's keep watching and listening," he said, his grip on my hand tightening protectively. "We'll find the truth, Robin. Together."

And as the night wore on, cloaked in darkness and intrigue, we danced a delicate dance – slipping through the shadows, gathering secrets and whispers, seeking the answers that would finally set us free. As we slipped into the shadows, I couldn't help but think of Belinda and Jim, working diligently to gather their own pieces of the puzzle. I prayed they would find something, anything, that would help us untangle the web of deceit and lies.

A woman's laughter rang out across the dimly lit ballroom, her beautiful face a mask of enjoyment. I didn't know who she was, but I marveled at her practiced grace, snatching at drinks from passing waiters and engaging those around her in light, seemingly careless conversation. Who was she? And why did she seem so comfortable in a room that was full of cruel killers? I was drawn to her and moved closer, but not too close.

"Hey, Nellie," one of the men slurred, placing a heavy hand on her hip. "You hear anything about that shipment coming in?"

"Can't say I have, Mickey," Nelly replied, expertly deflecting his touch as she put a new glass in his hand. "But you know how it is around here always something going on."

My heart raced with anticipation as I tucked away the tidbit of information, knowing it could prove valuable in our quest for truth.

Asa guided me through the crowd like a shadow, his blond hair and gray eyes betraying nothing about why I was there. He navigated the labyrinth of people and tables, stopping to chat with people he knew, seeking out any hint of information about what was going on. I watched him, almost afraid at how good he was at this. He was used to betraying people, good at hearing information, and comfortable living a lie. What did that say about him? Nothing I didn't already know.

"Hey, Asa," a young man called out, beckoning him closer. "Heard you were around. What's up?"

"Not much, James," Jim muttered, pushing his hands

into the pockets of his suit pants and casting a wary glance around the room. "You got any news for me, kid?"

"Maybe," the man replied, lowering his voice. "Word is there's been some movement down at the docks lately, late-night meetings, hushed conversations. Could be something worth looking into."

"Thanks, kid," Asa said, clapping the young officer on the shoulder before disappearing back into the shadows of the mansion on the outskirts of New Orleans. We walked away from the kid, but I could see the way his mind raced with possibilities, wondering if this new lead could bring us closer to exposing Declan's connection to my mother and sister's deaths.

In the quiet moments, I found myself reflecting on the tangled web we had become entwined in. The need for vengeance burned within me, fueled by the hatred I held for Declan. I wondered though, as we clung to the shadows, if I could trust Asa? Despite the growing intimacy between us, a gnawing uncertainty persisted, wrapping its icy tendrils around my heart.

"Are we doing the right thing?" I whispered to him, staring out at the gathered jet set of New Orleans. "Can we really expose Declan without putting ourselves, and everyone we care about, in danger?"

"Sweetheart, I wish I could promise you that everything will be okay," Asa murmured, his breath warm against my ear. "But all I can say is that we have to try. For your mom, for Angela, and for all those who have suffered at Declan's hands."

～

MINUTES PASSED, then hours, and I started to feel as if I was living in a dream. Or perhaps a nightmare would be more accurate. There was a melancholic haze that hung over us like a shroud, despite the festive atmosphere, a constant reminder of the danger that lurked around every corner, waiting to consume us in its merciless embrace. And though we didn't know what the future held, we carried on, driven to find answers that might kill us both.

Asa guided me to a balcony, took out a cigarette and lit it. He exhaled slowly, his mind lost in the things he'd heard. I looked around the property, unsettled by the people inside and the history that came with a home like the one the charity ball was held in. The humid night air clung to my skin like a heavy blanket, the scent of rain-soaked earth and decaying flowers filling my nostrils. Asa's fingers intertwined with mine, his grip both comforting and suffocating as we made our way through the house, listening to conversations from the shadows.

"I don't know how much more of this I can take," I whispered, my voice almost too quiet, but he nodded so he must have heard me.

"Just a little while longer," Asa replied, his voice equally hushed. "We'll go soon."

When we went back inside, the conversations had changed from whispered secret questions and answers to tales that made the listener laugh. We would get no more answers here tonight. Asa steered me towards the door, his hand on the elegant, dark olive-green evening gown I wore. It was a backless, silk number so his hand was high on my bottom, but I didn't mind. I looked over at him, dressed in a black suit and tie, and admired just how good he looked.

Asa drove us into the heart of the city, the tension growing palpable. His unease matched mine, I caught glimpses of it when we exchanged glances. The information we had uncovered in recent days painted a chilling picture of Declan's reach, one that extended far beyond the sordid confines of the Irish mafia.

We reached the café we'd all agreed to meet at, and Asa led me over to the table. We all looked rather grim as Asa and I took our seats. The mood wasn't high at all.

"Declan has eyes everywhere," Jim muttered, his weathered face drawn into a grimace that spoke volumes about the weight of his years in law enforcement. "We'll have to be careful not to leave any traces."

"Agreed," Belinda added, her innocent appearance belying the calculating mind that lay beneath. "It's going to take all of us working together if we want to bring him down."

The sultry air clung to my skin like a lover's embrace, and the aroma of chicory coffee filled the tiny cafe as we sat huddled around a small table. Belinda's eyes were wide with fear, but her voice held steady as she relayed the critical information she'd managed to gather from eavesdropping at the bar. With each word, I could feel the weight of her sacrifice, the risks she had taken to be our ally.

"Declan's reach is far greater than we anticipated," Belinda said, her voice low. "He has people in every corner of this city, even within the police force."

Jim listened intently, his tired eyes reflecting years of navigating the treacherous waters of law enforcement. He was a seasoned detective with a no-nonsense attitude, and his unexpected partnership with us was born out of mutual need. Declan's influence had grown too strong to ignore, and Jim's expertise would be vital for our success.

"I had a feeling that was the case, but I hoped it wouldn't turn out that way." He sighed, scrubbing a hand over his tired face. The lines were deeper this evening, or maybe that was the result of the shadows.

"Belinda," I whispered, my heart aching at the sight of her trembling hands, "you've done well. Thank you."

Her brown eyes met mine, and a soft smile graced her delicate features. "I made a promise to you, and I'll do whatever it takes to help you."

"You're very brave, Belinda," Asa added, his words carrying the weight of his gratitude.

Jim leaned forward, resting his elbows on the worn tabletop. "We're going to need to stay one step ahead of Declan if we want any chance at bringing him down. I have contacts who can help us, but we must tread carefully."

My stomach churned at the thought of delving deeper into the dark world that had swallowed the two people I loved the most. But there was no turning back now. The truth demanded to be uncovered, and we were the only ones who could bring it to light.

"Robin, I know this isn't easy for you," Jim said, his gaze heavy with empathy. "Have you found out anything more about him?"

"Nothing that's concrete. We heard a lot of people asking about some 'shipment' Declan has coming in but we don't know what it is, or when it's coming. Or if it even matters."

"I did learn that he's connected with the mob in New York. Some syndicate up there. Guy that runs it is called Nick Afonsi. I would say the last thing we need is a bunch of mobsters from New York coming down here, but Declan is greedy. We might be able to use that to bring him down." Asa said, not looking at me, but his leg brushed against mine, reassuring me he was still there, still needed me.

"Of course," I replied, my resolve solidifying like molten

steel cooling into hardened armor. "We'll do whatever it takes."

"Good," Jim nodded. "In the meantime, Belinda and I will continue to gather information from our respective sources. We need to move quickly, but discreetly."

"Time is not on our side," Asa agreed, his hand reaching for mine beneath the table, grounding me in the storm that threatened to swallow us whole.

It was hard work to peel back the layers of deceit and corruption that encased Declan's organization like a serpent's constricting coils. Moonlight filtered through the windows, casting a cold, white glow on the worn wooden table where we gathered. Asa's fingers were interlaced with mine, their comforting strength a silent reminder that we were in this together.

"Declan has been making some unusual moves lately," Belinda said, bringing our focus on her. "He's consolidating power, bringing in new players from outside the city. It seems like he's preparing for something big."

"It does," I said, worry putting a hard edge on my voice. "I don't know what any of that means, but it can't be good."

Asa squeezed my hand, his own report ready on his lips. "He's definitely hiding something, but it's not easy to get a read on him. He's a master of deception, keeping his true intentions shrouded in darkness."

My own contribution felt small in comparison to their daring exploits, but it was just as important.

"I've managed to get some information from a friend in New York, she can get into financial records and things that I can't, and she sent me a huge stack of paper this morning," I revealed, my fingers trembling as I recalled the endless hours spent parsing through layers of financial subterfuge.

"There's evidence of money laundering, payoffs to police, and connections to illegal activities that reach far beyond New Orleans."

Jim's tired eyes bore into mine, the weight of his years in law enforcement heavy on his shoulders.

"And my sources within the police force have confirmed your findings," he added, his voice gravelly and worn. "There are ongoing investigations into several members of Declan's organization, but they're being stonewalled at every turn. I suspect his reach goes much farther than the police. I'm surprised you were able to get anything on him at all."

My eyebrows went up a little, but I smiled at Jim. "Don't doubt the power of a determined woman with connections in the world of snooping."

I heard everyone chuckle at my little joke, and sighed. It was hard being a woman in a world ruled by men, but those of us that were determined found our own ways around the roadblocks often thrown up to pen us in. We were closer than ever to uncovering the truth about Declan's connection to my mom and sister's deaths, yet it seemed that with each new revelation, more questions arose, casting shadows over our fragile hope.

"Whatever we do," I whispered, unable to shake the feeling that we were walking a razor-thin edge between justice and oblivion, "we need to be careful. The deeper we delve into this world, the greater the danger becomes."

I went quiet then, exhausted, out of ideas, and uncertain as to what the future held. At some point, Declan would probably realize who I reminded him of, or he would find out what we were all up to. I wanted to go home, back to New York, but Asa had started to mean something to me. I didn't want it to end, even if disappearing, leaving all of these wonderful people behind, would be the best idea I ever had. I just couldn't do it. I'd promised them I was all in, and I meant it. I just don't know how long I'll live to prove it.

12

Robin

The icy touch of the air conditioner made me shiver as I leaned my head against Asa's broad shoulder, feeling the comforting rise and fall of his chest. We were sitting on the worn leather couch in the dimly lit living room of his house, a temporary haven from the chaos outside. In that moment, time seemed to slow down, and I allowed myself to forget the darkness of our pasts. Despite everything, I felt safe and protected in Asa's strong arms.

"Tell me something I don't know about you," I whispered, tracing circles on his hand with my fingertips. I wanted to be closer to him, to know everything about him. Maybe if I drew him closer to me, the doubts and worries I had about him would vanish into thin air. "Tell me another happy memory you hold dear.

Asa paused for a moment, lost in thought.

"There was this time when I took my little sister to the fair for the first time." He smiled, the corners of his gray eyes crinkling. "She was so excited, her eyes wide with wonder at all the bright lights and sounds. She held my hand so tight, like she never wanted to let go."

I smiled, picturing the scene in my mind. My heart ached for the innocence we had both lost along the way, but I held onto the hope that perhaps one day, we could find it again.

"Your turn," Asa said softly, pulling me closer.

"Oh. My mom used to take my sister and I to the beach at sunset." I closed my eyes, savoring the memory. "The sand was warm beneath my feet, and the waves kissed the shore with a gentle sigh. We built a bonfire, and as the sun dipped below the horizon, the sky bled into a dozen colors, golds, purples, and reds, intertwining like silk ribbons."

"Okay, now I know you're a writer. You just painted an image with words," Asa teased me before he tickled my lowers ribs, making me yell with feigned affront.

Asa and I continued to exchange stories, fragments of our lives that we clung to in this uncertain world. For a brief moment, we dared to dream of a future where the shadows of the past could no longer reach us. We weren't stupid, or oblivious. We were both aware that the scent of danger hung in the air, a palpable tension that made every nerve in my body scream for me to run, most of the time. Yet I remained rooted to the spot, unwilling, or unable, to leave Asa's side.

Later that night, we were on our way back to his house after dinner when a man stepped out of the shadows, his expression unreadable. I could see he was tall, blond, his skin tanned. A gold god. Then it hit me. Was this the golden god with a penthouse Angela escaped from?

"Evening, Asa," Eamon said, his voice smooth and chilling. I shivered involuntarily, feeling like a hunted animal caught beneath the predator's unwavering gaze. His eyes were dark, beady, cruel, and his mouth was a red slash, an incision more than a smile. I shivered again and stepped closer to Asa.

"Can we help you with anything, Eamon?" Asa asked, his voice steady despite the unease that flickered behind his eyes. His hand slipped into mine, offering comfort and reassurance as we faced this intimidating man.

"Actually, there is something." Eamon leaned in closer, his cold dark blue eyes boring into Asa's. "I've been watching you two for a while now. I must say, it's quite the interesting little romance you've got going on."

My heart thundered in my chest, pounding so violently that I feared it might burst through my ribs. Dread coiled around me like a serpent, its venomous fangs sinking deep into my soul. How could he have known? We hadn't hidden our relationship, but I've never seen the man before. That, obviously, didn't mean he hadn't seen me.

Asa's grip tightened around my hand, his jaw clenched as he struggled to maintain his composure. "What do you want, Eamon?"

"Isn't it obvious?" Eamon said, his voice dripping with malice. "I want to know what you're planning to do about it."

"About what?" Asa challenged, refusing to back down despite the clear threat looming over us.

"About your precious Robin here," Eamon sneered, casting a disdainful glance in my direction. "You know as well as I do that Declan won't take kindly to this little...dalliance. Or to finding out she's not just a tourist sucking your dick. She's one of his former whore's sister."

I lunged towards him, but Asa pulled me back, his eyes not on me, but on Eamon. His gaze flickered between Eamon and me, his thoughts a turbulent storm that raged behind the windows of his soul. I could see the indecision weighing heavily upon him, a burden he had not expected to bear so soon. And as the silence stretched between us like a taut wire, I knew that we were standing on the edge of an abyss, one misstep away from being swallowed by darkness.

"Leave her out of this, Eamon," Asa finally said, his voice barely more than a whisper.

"Out of the question," Eamon replied, his icy smile sending shivers down my spine. "You know the stakes, Asa. You know what will happen if you don't play along."

I watched helplessly as Asa's gaze flicked to the ground, his shoulders sagging with resignation. His voice, when it came, was hollow, the sound of a man who had seen too much and sacrificed even more. "Fine, Eamon. What do you want?"

"Information," Eamon said simply. "Details about Declan's operations. Anything that might give us an advantage."

"Us?" I couldn't help but interject, my voice trembling with fear and anger. "You mean you and whoever else is pulling your strings."

"Watch your tongue, girl," Eamon warned, his glare darkening with menace. "Or you'll find yourself in a world of pain."

"Eamon," Asa cut in, his voice firm. "I'll do what you want, but you leave Robin alone. Understand?"

Eamon considered Asa for a moment before nodding slowly.

"Very well. But remember, Asa, I'll be watching. One wrong move, and everything comes crashing down." With that, he turned and disappeared into the shadows, leaving us to face the uncertain future that now loomed before us.

I stood there, my heart pounding in my chest, as Eamon's threat echoed through my mind. I knew that if

Declan found out about who I was, the consequences would be dire for both of us. The tension in the air was palpable, and I could see the indecision flickering behind Asa's gray eyes.

"Come on, Asa," Eamon taunted, his voice dripping with malice. "Are you going to betray your little lover here or risk everything for her?"

Asa clenched his fists, his jaw tight with barely contained anger. I could see the weight of his decision reflected in the creases on his forehead and the beads of sweat gathering at his temples. He opened and closed his mouth, struggling to find the words to express the turmoil within him.

"Let me make it easier for you," Eamon continued, his icy gaze never leaving Asa's face. "If you don't cooperate, I'll expose your secret about who she really is to Declan. That means not only will he take care of Robin here," he gestured towards me with a sneer, "he'll destroy you as well. Completely. I'm talking annihilation, Asa. Everything will burn."

The threat seemed to hit Asa like a physical blow. His shoulders sagged, and I could feel the power shift in Eamon's favor. Eamon's cunning had struck its mark, and it was tearing Asa apart inside.

"Please, Asa," I whispered, reaching out to touch his arm. "You don't have to do this. We can find another way."

He looked at me, his gray eyes clouded with pain and uncertainty. In that moment, I saw the man beneath the hardened exterior, vulnerable, afraid, and struggling to do what was right.

"Robin," he murmured, and I could hear the regret in his voice. "I can't let anything happen to you. You know I can't."

I nodded, tears pricking at my eyes as I tried to swallow the lump in my throat. I knew the stakes were high, but watching Asa wrestle with his loyalties tore at my heart.

"Very well," Eamon said, a triumphant smile curling his lips. "You have your choice, Asa. Get me information or I destroy you both."

The silence that followed was deafening. I could feel the weight of both our fates hanging in the balance, and the seconds stretched into an eternity. My breath hitched as I waited for Asa's response, desperate for him to find a way out of this impossible situation.

Finally, with a heavy sigh, Asa spoke. "Alright, Eamon. I'll do it. I'll find out what I can for you."

The words cut through me like a knife, and I wondered if this would put us all in jeopardy. Who was this man? He must have some kind of power, some sway that went beyond spreading rumors. My heart shattered for Asa. I knew that Asa had made the only choice he could. In the end, family was everything, and neither of us could escape the ties that bound us to our pasts.

Eamon's cold laughter filled the air, and I shivered, wrapping my arms around myself as I stared at the man who was my lover. The future was uncertain, and danger lurked around every corner. But for now, we had no choice but to play our parts in this twisted game, praying that somehow, we would find a way to survive.

Eamon's eyes bored into me like icicles, his gaze never wavering as he spoke. "I want information on Declan's operations, Asa. Everything you can find."

I clenched my fists at my sides, feeling the sweat pool in my palms. The pressure was mounting, like a vice tightening around my chest. My heart raced, a desperate struggle for escape from this trap we were caught in.

"And if we can't get you that information?" I asked, my voice barely above a whisper.

"Then I'll make sure everyone knows about who you are, Robin," Eamon replied, a sinister smile playing on his lips. "And we both know what that would mean for you and Asa."

My mind swirled with images of Angela, her laughter echoing through my memories, her touch still lingering on my skin. The thought twisted inside me, gnawing at my insides like an untamed beast. But Asa's life his safety was everything. "I'll help him."

"Good," Eamon replied, his grin widening. "You have one week. Remember, Asa, I'm always watching."

As he walked away, I felt the air grow colder, the shadows of the alleyway seeming to close in around me. My legs shook beneath me, barely able to support the weight of the cross I now bore. The world had become a treacherous maze, filled with secrets and lies that threatened to consume us all. In that moment, I realized how fragile our lives truly were, teetering on the edge of a precipice with no escape in sight.

That night, as I lay beside Asa, I couldn't shake the feeling that we were teetering on the edge of an abyss, our relationship a flickering flame caught in the merciless winds of fate. I didn't want it to be. I wanted so much more time with him. To travel with him, to see the world, to experience everything with him.

The darkness was my veil, my shield from the memories that clawed at the edges of my mind. Beneath its cover, I sought out Asa's warmth, the solid comfort of his presence a balm to my frayed nerves. My hand moved with purpose, guided by an intimate knowledge of his sleeping form. The familiar heat of his skin under my fingertips sent a shiver down my spine.

I found him, that part of him that was thick, long, silky smooth even in the depths of sleep. He was unmoving now, but experience told me that stillness would soon be replaced with a stirring vitality. The room was silent, save for the sound of our breathing, mine quickening with anticipation.

With a steadiness borne from need, my fingers encircled him, gently coaxing him to hardness as I slid further down the cool sheets. My mouth hovered above him, the hunger inside me growing more insistent with each passing second. I thought of the pleasure he would give me, the way he always did when I offered myself like this. Asa had this uncanny ability to sense what I needed, often before I did myself. He gave willingly, passionately.

Tonight, it wasn't just about the physical release or the transient forgetting of a past that threatened to consume me. It was about owning these moments with him, savoring them like the last drops of a rare vintage that might never touch my lips again. With each breath, with every beat of my heart, I was claiming the present, living in the here and now that was Asa, dangerous, enigmatic Asa, whose ties to a world I barely understood both terrified and exhilarated me.

As my lips parted, ready to take him in, I allowed myself to drown in the sensations, to be consumed by the urgency of our connection. This was my escape, my mystery, my danger, and in these silent, desperate seconds, it was all that mattered.

Asa's groan rumbled through the darkness, a low sound that vibrated against my lips as they closed over him. His body reacted beneath me, his cock growing harder with each pull of my mouth, inch by deliberate inch. I savored the heat of him, the taste, the rawness of this connection.

"Robin, fuck, baby, you make me so hard," he whispered, the words barely a breath, yet they charged the air with an electric spark. The night cloaked us in its shadow, but Asa's voice was like a beacon, guiding me through the fog of my own longing.

I rose from my position, shifting to straddle him, feeling the coarse hair on his legs against my thighs. Sliding down onto him felt like coming home, something I hadn't truly felt in so long. My movements were frenzied, driven by a need that clawed at my insides with sharp, insistent talons.

His hands found my breasts, fingers grasping with a firmness that sent shivers down my spine. He shaped me, molded me, his touch igniting tiny fires that spread through my veins. Nipples pebbled under his touch as I plunged deeper into the haze of pleasure.

A hand trailed down my body, a lone explorer on a quest for that peak of ecstasy. Fingers circled my clit, coaxing it to life with the same urgency that pulsed within me. I rode the wave, let it crash over me, and under his powerful thrusts, I shattered, pieces of me scattering like stars across the sky of our joined bodies.

Breathless, I leaned down, my lips searching for his in the dark. Our kiss was a seal, a promise, a balm to the wounds of my past. When he finally came deep inside of me, it was as if he was filling those cracks, making me whole again.

In the stillness that followed, wrapped in the strength of his arms, I could finally let the world fade away. Sleep beckoned, a gentle whisper promising rest and refuge. And for a fleeting moment, nestled against Asa's chest, I believed I was safe. I had to believe it.

13

Robin

I watched the rain pour down the windows, the world outside gray and black. I'd given up my room at the motel now, and had settled into Asa's bedroom with him. Life was so precious now, the worry about people looking down their noses at us for living together when we weren't married, didn't really seem to matter. I wanted what time I could get with him. When he'd offered to let me move in, I'd agreed. For better or for worse.

His secluded house nestled in the heart of the city, hidden from prying eyes by a canopy of trees that surrounded it like a protective embrace. The air was heavy with anticipation and the scent of the rain pouring down outside. Asa stood by the window, his muscular frame cloaked in shadows, his gray eyes reflecting the moonlight that streamed through the cracked glass. He was deep in thought, no doubt contemplating how to take down Eamon Doyle and protect what remained of our families. His presence brought an odd sense of comfort, despite the danger that came with aligning ourselves against men like Declan and Eamon.

"Alright, everyone," Asa's voice cut through the room like a knife, "we need to come up with a solid plan. Robin, what do you think?"

"Precision and caution are crucial," I said, my brown eyes meeting those of our allies who filled the room. "We need to be smart about this. One wrong step, we could lose everything."

"Robin's right," Jim said, his voice low and steady. "Eamon has been deep in this game for years. We can't afford to underestimate him."

"We won't," I whispered, more to myself than anyone else. Memories of my family's tragic past haunted me, urging me to tread carefully, lest I become another casualty in this ruthless war.

"Then let's get to work," Asa said, his eyes never leaving mine. "We all have our roles to play, and we need to move quickly."

As we began outlining our strategy, the room seemed to close in around me, the walls whispering secrets of betrayal and loss. I tried to focus on the task at hand, but my thoughts kept drifting to the danger that lay ahead, the lives that hung in the balance.

"Robin?" Asa's voice pulled me from my reverie, his concern evident in the furrow of his brow. "Are you with us?"

I nodded, swallowing the lump in my throat.

"Yes," I whispered, my voice barely audible above the crackling of the fire. "I'm with you."

"Good," he said, offering me a reassuring smile that somehow managed to ease the storm inside me. "We'll get through this."

I could feel Asa's gaze on me, his gray eyes piercing through the darkness like a beacon of hope.

"Robin," he said gently, his voice warm and steady. "Do you believe me?"

"I don't know," I murmured, my voice quiet but unwavering. "You once said something along the lines of we make our own futures. But is that true? Do we really? Or is it already determined for us?"

Asa flashed me a smile that held both encouragement and understanding before he leaned down to kiss me. Belinda and Jim left us then, off to do what they could to keep gathering information for us. For Eamon too, I reminded myself, hugging my arms around my waist.

"It's not as bad as it seems, Robin," Asa said, coming over to sit down at my feet. He picked up one, massaging the spot that ached the most, making my eyes close as he eased the tension there. "We can do this."

I could only let him massage my foot and wait for whatever he wanted to say next.

"Okay," Asa started, his voice firm and authoritative. "We need to make sure this place is a fortress. No one gets in or out without us knowing about it."

"Agreed," I agreed. "We should reinforce the doors and windows but make sure we can get out, if we need to."

"Yes, that's good." Asa nodded, his gray eyes glinting with determination. "We also need to arm ourselves. Let's make sure we have enough weapons and ammunition if we need it."

As he set to work, I turned my attention to my own task: gathering crucial information about Eamon's operations. Infiltrating the Irish mafia's secrets wouldn't be easy, but I knew I had the resourcefulness and connections to dig deep into their world.

I reached for my address book, turning the pages until I found a familiar name that sent shivers down my spine. Jacob, a former lover who still had ties to the darker work to be done in New York City. It would be risky to involve him, but I couldn't ignore the potential value of his insight.

"Jacob," I said when he picked up the phone, my heart pounding in my chest. "It's Robin. I need your help."

"Robin," he replied cautiously, his voice betraying a hint of surprise. "It's been a long time. What do you need?"

"Information," I told him firmly. "I need to know more about Eamon Doyle's and Declan O'Sullivan's operations. Can you help me?"

There was a pause on the other end, and I could almost feel the weight of Jacob's hesitation. Finally, he sighed. "Alright, but we need to meet in person. I don't trust these lines."

"I'm not in New York," I answered, suppressing the shudder that ran through me at the thought of meeting him face-to-face. "If you don't trust the phones, mail it to me. Overnight it. I'll pay the cost."

As I hung up the phone, a thousand questions swirled in my mind. What secrets would Jacob reveal? Could I trust him not to betray us to Eamon? And how would Asa react if he knew I was taking such a risk?

"Robin?" Asa's voice broke through my thoughts, his gray eyes searching mine with concern. "Are you alright?"

"Fine," I replied, forcing a smile that felt as fragile as glass. "Just working on gathering information. I have a contact who may be able to help."

Asa nodded, his gaze never leaving mine.

"Be careful," he warned gently. "We can't afford any mistakes."

"I know," I murmured, my heart aching with the weight of our shared burden. "I promise I'll be cautious."

"I know you will, Robin." Asa's hand found mine, his fingers intertwining with mine in a gesture both comforting and protective. "But, over the last few weeks, you've become all I can think about, the only person I ever want to come home to. The woman I love. My reason to keep trying, especially now when things are so messed up. I just want to keep you safe. Is that too much to ask for?"

"Not at all," I whispered, clinging to the lifeline he offered me. I smiled at him, kissing the jawline I loved so very much. Even if it was still hard to admit. "I love you too, you know?"

"I know, Robin. It's what keeps me going." he replied, stroking my face tenderly. What would I do if these moments with him ever came to an end? I didn't want to think about it.

TWO DAYS LATER, Asa was out buying ammunition for the small armory he'd collected and I was in the kitchen. The only noise was the soft rustle of paper as I pored over the information Jacob sent down to me. Each page revealed a new horror, a new atrocity committed by Eamon and his accomplices. Drug trafficking, money laundering, human trafficking, the list went on and on. My heart pounded with each new revelation, my mind struggling to process the enormity of it all.

"Robin?"

Asa's voice broke through the stillness, his footsteps echoing off the walls. I looked up to see him standing before me, his eyes searching mine for answers.

"Anything?" he asked, his voice low and urgent.

I nodded, my throat too tight to speak.

"It's worse than we thought," I managed to whisper.

Asa's expression hardened, his jaw clenching with anger. "We have to use this. Find a way to weaken him."

"I know," I replied, my mind racing with possibilities. "But how? There's so much here, it's overwhelming."

"Start small," Asa advised, his hand finding mine once more. "Look for patterns. See where we can exploit their weaknesses."

I nodded again, my thoughts a jumbled mess. It was hard to think straight when every page seemed to reveal a new horror. But Asa was right. We had to find a way to use this information, to turn it against Eamon and Declan.

"You want to read through some of this?" I offered, dividing the stack in half.

"Sure," Asa said, taking a seat across from me.

Together, we hunched over the papers, analyzing each page with a critical eye. The tension in the room was palpable, each of us acutely aware of the danger that lurked outside these walls.

"Wait," I said suddenly, my finger pointing to a line on the page. "This could be it."

Asa leaned in closer, his eyes scanning the words. "What is it?"

"All of," I said, my heart racing with excitement. "Declan's been funneling funds through a shell corporation for years. If we can expose that, it could cripple him. In the process, it could take down Eamon."

Asa smiled, his eyes alight with a fierce determination. "Who do we contact? The FBI?"

I nodded, a surge of adrenaline coursing through me. This was it. Our chance to strike back against the man who had taken so much from us. "Maybe. Right now, let's see if we can appease Eamon with this. I'll make copies of it and give those to him. Let him take down Declan, and then we go after him. Or the other way around, whichever works out in our favor."

Asa nodded, seeing the logic of my plan. Now, it just had to work out for us. Otherwise, we might end up doomed.

THE NIGHT AIR was thick with the scent of impending rain, and the shadows cast by the towering warehouses created an eerie landscape for the plan we were about to set in motion. Asa and I stood on a dimly lit rooftop, the worn concrete beneath our feet damp from the day's earlier drizzle. The city sprawled out before us, its twinkling lights a reminder of the lives we were fighting to protect.

"Are you sure this is going to work?" I asked quietly, my heart pounding in my chest as I glanced over at him.

Asa's gray eyes met mine, the intensity of his gaze sending shivers down my spine.

"It has to," he replied, his voice steady despite the danger that lurked ahead. "We can't let either of them get away with what they've done."

I nodded, unable to shake the image of the pages filled with Declan and Eamon's dark secrets. We needed more something a little more, more evidence, something definitive that would allow us to bring him down for good.

"Alright," I said, taking a deep breath as I steeled myself for the task ahead. "What do we know about this meeting?"

Asa leaned against the crumbling brick wall behind him, his muscular arms crossed over his broad chest.

"It's a gathering of high-ranking members of the Irish

mafia," he explained, his voice low and measured. "They're discussing their next big move, which means they'll be sharing critical information with each other."

"Information that could be invaluable to us," I added, my determination to see this through growing stronger by the second.

"Exactly," he agreed, his lips curving into a half-smile that somehow seemed more dangerous than reassuring. "Now, as for getting us in there..."

"Your connections?" I prompted, remembering how entwined Asa was with this world we sought to dismantle.

"Right," he said, pushing off the wall and taking a step toward me. "I've arranged for us to attend under the guise of emissaries from another branch of the organization. We'll have to be careful, but it should give us the cover we need."

"Are you sure we can trust them?" I asked, my voice barely above a whisper.

"Trust is a luxury we don't have," he replied, his eyes never leaving mine. "But they have as much to gain from Eamon's downfall as we do."

I swallowed hard, knowing that this was our only shot at infiltrating the meeting without raising suspicion.

"Okay," I said, trying to keep the tremor out of my voice. "Let's do this."

Asa reached out and gently took my hand, giving it a reassuring squeeze.

"We've come this far, Robin," he murmured, his breath warm against my cheek. "We can do this."

His words were like a lifeline in the darkness, grounding me and reminding me why we had chosen to walk this treacherous path. For our families, for justice, and for each other.

With a final nod, we turned our gazes toward the

building where Declan's meeting would soon take place. My heart pounded relentlessly in my chest, each beat echoing the gravity of our mission. Asa had called in favors to secure us an invitation to Declan's secret meeting, and now, here we were, on the precipice of danger.

"Remember," Asa whispered as he leaned in, his gray eyes steady on mine. "You're Siobhan O'Reilly, a high-ranking member of the rival gang. Don't hesitate if they test you. They'll sniff out any weakness."

I nodded, trying to quiet the storm of fear brewing within me. The weight of the small, concealed gun against my hip served as a reminder that we were walking into the lion's den, but it also gave me a sense of power, steeling my resolve. Jim and Belinda waited at a safe distance, prepared to intervene if things went south.

I touched the blond wig on my head, making sure it hadn't slipped. Another touch pushed the glasses I'd bought at a drug store up my nose a little. I hoped the gesture didn't smudge the eyeliner and eyeshadow I'd applied in just the right way to hide the natural shape of my eyes. It was the best I could do as a disguise.

"Let's go," I murmured, and with that, we stepped through the heavy doors of the warehouse where Declan's meeting was taking place.

Inside, the dimly lit room reeked of stale smoke and the metallic tang of blood. Men and women clad in dark attire congregated in clusters, their hushed conversations punctuated by the occasional cruel laugh. I felt the heat of their gazes on us, scrutinizing and calculating, as we navigated the dangerous atmosphere. Eamon's loyal and ruthless associates surrounded us, waiting for any sign of deception.

"Siobhan," a gravelly voice greeted us, pulling me from my thoughts. A tall, burly man with a scarred face approached, extending his hand to me. I shook it firmly, masking the tremor in my grip with a forced smile. "Heard quite a bit about you."

"Likewise," I replied, my voice steady despite the pounding in my ears. "Declan's reputation precedes him."

"Indeed, it does," he said, his eyes narrowing as they flicked to Asa. He had on a dark brown wig, an awful mustache, and brown tinted glasses. To me he still looked like Asa, just a bad version of him, but we hoped it would fool Declan and his men, if any of them looked at him at all. "And who is this?"

"Brian, an associate of mine," I answered, feeling the heat of Asa's reassuring presence beside me. "He's here to observe and learn."

"Very well," the man grunted, stepping aside to let us pass deeper into the warehouse.

As we moved through the crowd, my senses were flooded with the sounds of hushed whispers and clinking glasses. The tension was palpable, a heavy fog that threatened to choke me. I could feel the weight of their stares, each one like a blade pressing against my skin, daring me to falter.

"Stay close," Asa murmured, his breath warm against my ear. "We can't afford any missteps tonight."

"I know," I whispered back, my eyes scanning the room for Eamon. The stakes were impossibly high, and the knowledge of what hung in the balance made my heart ache with a mixture of fear and longing. We had ventured so far into this labyrinth of danger, and now all that remained was to find our way out, together.

But first, we had to face the monsters at the center of it all: Eamon Doyle and Declan O'Sullivan.

The murmurs of conversation swirled around me like

smoke, carrying secrets I desperately needed to unlock. Asa and I navigated the dimly lit warehouse, the scent of stale alcohol and cigarette smoke filling my nostrils. The floorboards creaked beneath our feet as we moved through the sea of Declan's associates, each one a potential threat.

"Stick close," Asa whispered in my ear, his breath warm and comforting amidst the chilling atmosphere. I nodded, maintaining my facade of confidence. His presence was both a shield and an anchor, giving me the courage to delve deeper into this treacherous world.

I listened intently, straining to catch snippets of conversations as they floated past. "...shipment arriving tomorrow...", "...new territory...", "... Declan doesn't trust..." Every word was another piece of the puzzle, another clue to Declan's plans.

My eyes darted around the room, searching for Declan himself. There, at the far end of the warehouse, he stood surrounded by a group of his most trusted men. His dark hair gleamed in the muted light, and his icy gaze seemed to pierce through the darkness, locking onto mine for a moment before flicking away. My heart skipped a beat, but I forced myself to stay calm, reminding myself that Asa was with me.

As I watched Declan, I could see the way his subordinates deferred to him, their shoulders hunched and gazes averted. They hung on to his every word, fearful of displeasing him. It was clear that Declan held all the power here, and understanding the dynamics of his relationships would be key to dismantling his operation.

"Robin," Asa murmured, drawing me back to the present. "Remember, don't linger too long. We don't want to raise suspicion."

"Of course," I replied, forcing a small smile. His mere

presence beside me allowed me to move through the crowd without attracting too much attention. I had a man with me, and none of the other men would bother me while he was with me.

The air grew thick with tension, the acrid scent of cigar smoke burning my nostrils as I listened to the hushed conversations around me. My heart pounded in my chest, a relentless drumbeat echoing the urgency of our mission. As the meeting progressed, I paid close attention to any slip of information that could lead us closer to Declan's undoing.

"Have you heard about the shipment coming in next week?" one man whispered to another, his voice barely audible above the low hum of voices.

We'd been hearing that this shipment was on the way for quite a while now. Each day, however, the timeframe of this shipment's arrival seemed to get pushed back. That made me wonder if anything was actually coming or if Declan just liked keeping the rumor-mill going.

"Of course," the other replied, casting a sidelong glance towards Declan across the room. "It's going to be a game-changer."

"Keep quiet about it, though," the first man warned. "Declan doesn't want anyone knowing the specifics."

"Robin," Asa murmured into my ear, his breath warm against my skin. "I have a bad feeling. We should start making our way out."

"Right," I agreed, nodding as I discreetly scanned the room for an exit. My mind raced, thoughts tangled like vines as I clung to the hope that we had gathered enough information to put a dent in Declan's operation.

"Let's go," he suggested, his hand resting on the small of my back, guiding me through the throng of dangerous men.

The deceptive calm of his touch belied the storm brewing beneath his placid exterior.

With each step toward the exit, my heart raced alongside the ticking clock, counting down the moments until we could breathe easy once more. As the door closed behind us, sealing away the world of deception and danger, I let out a shaky breath I hadn't realized I'd been holding.

"Are you alright?" Asa asked, his gray eyes searching mine for any signs of distress.

"Yes," I replied, my voice barely above a whisper. "We made it out."

14

Robin

The rain drizzled softly against the windowpane, creating a soothing rhythm that filled the dimly lit room. I found myself in Asa's house, surrounded by the shadows dancing on the walls from the flickering candlelight. It was an intimate and vulnerable space, one that allowed us to truly see each other without any pretenses or barriers.

"Here, sit down," Asa said, guiding me gently to the plush sofa. His touch sent shivers down my spine, making my heart race with anticipation. His gray eyes held mine, full of warmth and tenderness, as he handed me a glass of red wine.

"Thank you," I murmured, taking a sip and allowing the rich flavor to envelop my senses. The taste of the wine mirrored the bittersweet emotions that had brought us together, a blend of passion and pain, love and loss.

Asa leaned against the wall, watching me, standing far away. What was he up to, I wondered, taking another sip of the wine with a delighted smile. I liked the casual way he posed there and wished I had a camera with me so I could take a picture of him. He smiled as mine became a grin.

"What's amusing you so much?" Asa asked, pulling his glass to his lips as he came to sit down beside me on the couch.

"Nothing, I just like looking at you. Is that so bad?" I raised my eyebrows in question, but the grin was still in place.

"Not at all, I just wanted to be sure I didn't have toilet paper sticking out of my pants or something," he leaned over then, kissing me softly before he pulled away.

"No, no toilet paper. Just you in all your glory," I replied running my fingers into his blond hair, loving how silky it was. Hoping he'd do all the dirty things to me again that he knew I loved. I dearly loved how good he was at distracting me.

"Your strength is incredible, Robin," Asa whispered, his voice laced with admiration. "You've been through so much, yet you don't give up."

I felt a blush creep up my cheeks at his words, but I couldn't deny how they made me feel. As if every wound I carried was suddenly worth bearing, knowing that Asa saw something special in me despite them. It was a connection I'd never experienced before, an intertwining of our souls that transcended physical attraction.

"Thank you, Asa," I replied softly, our gaze locked. "And your loyalty and devotion to those you care about is something I truly admire."

He smiled, his disarming grin making my heart flutter.

"You're worth fighting for, Robin," he said earnestly, causing the air around us to hum with electricity.

The boundaries between us blurred as we leaned in

closer, our breaths mingling and our hearts pounding. I closed my eyes and let myself be swept away by the intensity of the moment, feeling Asa's lips brush against mine in a tender yet passionate kiss that sent shockwaves through my body. Our hands found each other in the darkness, fingers interlocking as he leaned over me.

In that blissful moment, as the rain continued to fall outside and the candlelight flickered on our entwined forms, all the pain and heartache from our pasts seemed to dissolve into the ether. It was as if our souls had finally found solace in one another, a refuge from the storms that raged within and around us. And for the first time in what felt like an eternity, I allowed myself to believe that maybe, just maybe, I could find happiness amidst the chaos of this life.

The blissful connection between Asa and I lingered, filling me with a warmth that had nothing to do with the temperature outside. I found myself cherishing his warm embrace, allowing it to cocoon me from life's harsh realities. But as the silence stretched on, an unspoken whisper of unease began to slither through my thoughts, casting a shadow over the happiness that had momentarily bloomed.

"Hey," Asa's voice broke the spell, his grey eyes locking onto mine with a glimmer of concern. "What's going on in that beautiful head of yours?"

I shook my head, trying to dispel the growing storm cloud.

"Nothing," I lied, forcing a smile. "Just...lost in thought."

"About what?" he pressed, his thumb gently stroking the back of my hand.

"Everything," I admitted, my gaze drifting towards the rain-streaked window. The droplets raced each other down the glass, their paths intertwining and diverging, much like our own lives, tossed about by fate's cruel hand.

"Robin," Asa said softly, his fingers tilting my chin back to face him. "You can tell me anything, you know that, right?"

"Of course," I murmured, though my heartstrings tightened with uncertainty. Could I truly trust this man who had entered my life like a whirlwind, stirring up long-buried emotions and memories? I wanted to believe he was genuine, that we could find solace in our shared pain and love. Yet, a nagging doubt still clung to the edges of my consciousness, refusing to be silenced.

A knock at the front door had Asa racing out of bed and through the house. At this point, it could be anyone, but he'd promised to keep me safe. He took it seriously.

As if on cue, the sound of hushed voices floated through the closed bedroom door. My senses on alert, I strained to listen, curiosity piqued by the clandestine conversation taking place just beyond our sanctuary.

"–I thought we agreed to keep this from her," one voice hissed, the tone urgent and familiar. "The last thing she needs is more heartache."

"Trust me, I never wanted her involved in any of this," Asa's voice replied, heavy with regret. "But the truth has a way of coming out, and I'd rather she heard it from me than someone else."

"Even if that truth could destroy everything you've built together?" the other voice challenged.

"Especially then," Asa conceded, his words laden with pain. "She deserves to know."

My breath caught in my throat as the implications of their exchange settled like lead in my gut. What secret was Asa hiding?

I stared at him from behind the cracked, my mind racing with unanswered questions and unsettling suspicions. The man who had brought light into my darkness, who had made me feel alive again, was he truly who he appeared to be? Or was our connection merely another cruel illusion, destined to crumble under the weight of reality's harsh glare?

"Robin?" Asa called out and I opened the door. His eyes searched mine for an answer to the unspoken question that hung between us. But in that moment, I couldn't find the words.

I stood there, my heart pounding like a relentless drumbeat in my chest, the words I had overheard swirling together into an unfathomable storm of confusion and dread. It felt as though the entire world had come to a screeching halt, leaving me suspended in this moment, unable to move or breathe.

"Robin," Asa began cautiously, his voice barely more than a whisper. "Please, let me explain."

But I couldn't find it within me to respond. The shock and disbelief coursed through me like ice-cold water, numbing my senses and stifling any words that might have formed. My mind was a whirlwind of fractured memories and shattered dreams, the fragments cutting deep into the vulnerable recesses of my soul.

"What have you kept from me, Asa?" I finally choked out, so lost in a lifetime of pain that I couldn't see anything but a shattered heart in my future. That's how it always went, didn't it? A little bit of happiness, deem, crushing pain. A never-ending cycle.

"Robin, look at me," he pleaded, taking a tentative step toward me. His gray eyes were filled with an anguish I had never seen before, their piercing depths betraying the turmoil hidden beneath his rugged exterior. Whoever he'd been talking to was gone now. It was just us.

As he reached for my hand, I caught a glimpse of the remorse etched into the lines of his face, a testament to the guilt that weighed heavily upon him. He held my gaze, searching for some semblance of understanding, but all I could see was the reflection of my own pain mirrored back at me.

With a heavy sigh, Asa began to talk. "I was the one that sent Eamon to look for Angela. I didn't know she was a sister. I didn't know what he'd done. I didn't know Eamon was the one that bought her."

Pain squeezed at my heart, and I think I forgot how to breathe, but Asa wasn't finished.

"Declan told me she was the niece of a friend, someone that the uncle wanted to get back, for her own safety. I didn't know he was kidnapping and selling women. When I chose Eamon, I didn't know he'd bought her. I just thought he was one of Declan's followers. He had money, but he's always wanted to be this big shot gangster. I thought sending him to New York would get him out of our hair down here. I didn't know, Robin. I swear, I didn't know."

I stared at the ground, trying to catch my breath, trying to not launch myself at Asa. He sent Eamon? So, it was Eamon that killed my mom and sister then. And Declan had a hand in it too. That gave me some answers, anyway.

"Say something," he implored, the desperation in his voice tugging at the frayed edges of my resolve. "Anything."

My lips parted, as if to speak, but the words remained trapped within the confines of my throat, strangled by a tide of emotion that threatened to engulf me. With every fiber of my being, I wanted to believe that there was an explanation for the damning conversation I had overheard, that our love was not built upon a foundation of lies and deceit.

But as I looked into Asa's tormented eyes, I couldn't shake the gnawing sense of unease that had taken root in the depths of my heart. The whispers of doubt grew louder, drowning out any hope of redemption or reconciliation.

"Tell me," I finally managed to choke out, my voice trembling with suppressed tears. "Tell me it's not true."

Asa's expression crumpled, and for a moment, he seemed as if he was about to break down entirely. But he swallowed hard, steeling himself against the overwhelming tide of emotion.

"I never meant for this to happen," he whispered, his words laced with regret. "I didn't know, Robin. I swear to you, I didn't know."

The flickering candlelight danced upon the shadows of Asa's face, casting an eerie glow over the room as we sat there in a suffocating silence. The weight of our unspoken words seemed to fill every corner, leaving me with a sense of claustrophobia that threatened to consume me.

"Did you know?" I finally whispered, my voice barely audible above the pounding of my heart. "Did you know Eamon killed them before I came down here?"

Asa hesitated, his jaw tightening as he fought to find the right words.

"I knew he was dangerous, Robin," he admitted softly. "But I didn't know he was responsible for what happened to your family."

"Then why didn't you tell me?" I demanded, my anger and hurt spilling over into the space between us. "Why didn't you warn me about him?"

"Because I was afraid when I figured out who you were," he confessed, his gray eyes filled with sorrow. "Afraid that if I told you the truth, you'd turn away from me. That you'd never be able to see past the darkness that has always followed me. Declan took me in when my parents died in a drive-by shooting. He gave me a home, and his way of life is all I've ever known."

"Is that really all it is?" I asked, my voice trembling with doubt. "Or is there something else you're not telling me?"

Asa looked at me, his eyes imploring me to understand. "Robin, I would lay down my life for you. But there are some secrets that even I can't escape. And the truth is...I wasn't sure how deep this went until now."

"Then help me make sense of it," I said, my voice cracking under the strain of my emotions. "Help me understand how the man I love could have any part in the destruction of my family."

Asa reached for my hand, his touch warm and familiar despite the coldness that had settled within me.

"I promise you, Robin, I never wanted any of this," he said, his voice thick with emotion. "But sometimes we don't get to choose our path. Sometimes the darkness reaches out and claims us, even when all we want is to be free of it."

"Can I trust you, Asa?" I asked, my heart heavy with uncertainty. "Can I really trust that you won't betray me like you did my family?"

"Robin, there's not a moment that goes by where I don't wish I could change the past," he said, his eyes pleading with me to believe him. "And if I could take away your pain, I would do so in an instant. But all I can do now is fight for a future where we can both find peace."

"Is that even possible?" I wondered aloud, the weight of our shared history enveloping me like a shroud. "Can we ever truly escape the darkness that seems determined to tear us apart?"

"I don't know," Asa admitted, his voice tinged with sadness. "But I do know one thing: I will spend every last breath fighting for us, Robin. For the love that has changed me in ways I never thought possible."

As the shadows played across his face, I saw not only the pain of his past but the hope that burned within him. And though my heart was heavy with doubt and fear, I couldn't help but cling to that hope, the hope that maybe, just maybe, love could conquer all.

The air in Asa's house had grown thick, heavy with unspoken words and the ghosts of our pasts. An oppressive silence settled around us like a suffocating embrace, punctuated only by the distant hum of traffic outside. The dim light from the single lamp cast long shadows on the walls, each one a distorted reflection of the truth that now hung between us, and a constant reminder of the secrets we could no longer hide.

"Robin," Asa began, his voice rough, weighted down by the burden of our newfound reality. He reached out to me, fingers trembling ever so slightly, but I hesitated, my heart caught in my throat as I looked into his gray eyes, now clouded with doubt and fear.

"Please, just tell me what you're thinking," he implored, desperation tingeing his voice.

I swallowed hard, struggling to find the right words, to express the maelstrom of emotions raging within me. "I don't know if I can trust you, Asa. Not after everything I've learned."

"Robin, I swear to you, I never meant for any of this to happen," he said, his voice cracking under the strain. His gaze bored into mine, searching for understanding, begging for forgiveness.

My mind reeled with conflicting emotions, anger,

betrayal, sorrow, all threatening to consume me whole. Yet, beneath it all, there was still a whisper of desire, a lingering ache that refused to be silenced.

"Then prove it to me," I replied, my voice barely above a whisper, my resolve wavering as I stared into those stormy depths.

"I will," he vowed, determination etched across his rugged features. "I'll do whatever it takes to make this right."

As we stood there, the distance between us closing inch by agonizing inch, the night outside seemed to press against the windows, a silent witness to our struggle. The tension in the room was palpable, a living entity that threatened to swallow us whole.

"Robin, I love you," Asa breathed, his words like an anchor tethering me to him as he closed the distance between us. And yet, as his lips brushed against mine, a shiver ran down my spine, a premonition of danger that I couldn't quite shake.

A sudden knock at the door shattered the fragile moment, the sound echoing like a gunshot through the stillness of the room. We pulled apart instantly, our eyes locked in mutual shock and fear.

"Who is it?" I whispered, my heart pounding violently against my ribcage.

"I don't know," Asa replied, his voice tight with anxiety as he moved cautiously towards the door. "But whoever it is, I'll get rid of them."

As Asa's hand reached for the doorknob, I held my breath, bracing myself for whatever lay on the other side, and praying that my heart could weather the storm that had just begun.

15

Robin

The visitor had only been Belinda, stopping by to check on me. She stayed for 20 minutes, then left, leaving me with nothing else to do but go back to bed. The dim glow of a single candle flickered in the quiet room, casting shadows that danced on the walls like ghosts. I sat on the edge of the bed, my body tense with the weight of my loss and the uncertainty of the future. Asa stood near the window, his broad shoulders slumped as if carrying an invisible burden. The distant sound of raindrops falling against the glass pane only added to the somber atmosphere.

"Robin," Asa's voice was barely above a whisper, yet it cut through the silence like a knife. He moved closer, his gray eyes searching my face for understanding, for comfort. But I could not bring myself to meet his gaze, even though I knew my avoidance only increased the distance between us.

We were both physically and emotionally drained, our bodies worn from the constant struggle to keep moving forward, to survive. And yet, there we were, standing together in this small, dark room, unable or perhaps unwilling to find solace in each other's arms. My heart ached at the thought, but I couldn't shake the feeling that embracing him would be akin to surrendering a piece of myself, a piece that I wasn't sure I could afford to lose, not now.

"Talk to me, Robin," he implored, his strong hands trembling slightly as they reached out to touch the curve of my cheek. The warmth of his skin sent shivers down my spine, and for a moment, I allowed myself to be lost in the sensation, to forget the pain and confusion that threatened to consume me.

"Everything is so...heavy," I finally admitted, my voice barely audible. "I don't know how much more of this I can take."

Asa nodded solemnly, his gray eyes filled with a sadness that mirrored my own. He pulled me into his embrace, wrapping his strong arms around me protectively. I wanted to revel in the safety of his touch, but my body remained rigid, unwilling to give in completely.

"Robin," he whispered into my hair, "I wish there was something I could do to make it all go away."

"Me too," I replied softly, feeling the weight of our shared pain settle over us like a heavy blanket. As we stood there, holding each other in the flickering candlelight, the scent of rain and the distant sound of thunder seemed to echo the turmoil that raged within our hearts.

I leaned my head against Asa's chest, listening to the steady rhythm of his heartbeat. His arms were a sanctuary, but they couldn't erase the memories that haunted me. My thoughts drifted back to the events that led us here, the betrayals and bloodshed, the secrets we'd unearthed, and the love that had blossomed amidst the chaos.

"Is it worth it?" I asked quietly, my voice barely audible above the sound of raindrops tapping against the window-panes. "All this pain and danger...for us?"

Asa hesitated, his breathing hitching slightly. He seemed to be searching for the right words, as if trying to pluck them from the shadows of the dimly lit room.

"Robin," he began, his voice laced with vulnerability, "I never wanted any of this for you. I didn't know that my connection to the Irish mafia would bring such tragedy into your life."

His fingers traced circles on my back, sending shivers down my spine.

"But when I look into your eyes, I see something worth fighting for. Something worth risking everything for." The intensity of his gaze held me captive, his gray eyes reflecting the storm that brewed outside.

"Can you forgive me, Robin?" he continued, his voice breaking with emotion. "For the part I played in your family's tragedy? I can't bear the thought of losing you. I know I've hurt you, and I'll do whatever it takes to make it right. I swear it on my life."

Tears welled in my eyes as I considered his words, weighed down by the enormity of the decision before me. Could I truly forgive him? And if so, could our love survive the darkness that still threatened to consume us?

"Time will tell, Asa," I whispered, my heart heavy with uncertainty and longing. "Time will tell."

The flickering candlelight cast eerie shadows on the walls, heightening the uncertainty that consumed me. I could hear the distant sound of rain outside, its rhythmic patter a melancholy accompaniment to the heaviness in my heart. The air around us felt thick and oppressive, as if it too bore the weight of our unspoken fears.

"Robin," Asa's voice broke through the silence, tentative and laced with emotion. "I need you to know how much I love you. I would do anything to protect you."

His words echoed in my mind, clashing with the bitter memories of pain he had inadvertently caused. My heart raced, torn between the fierce love that bound us together and the anguish that threatened to tear us apart.

"Can we ever truly move past this, Asa?" I asked, my voice barely a whisper. "Can we outrun the ghosts that haunt us?"

The hollowness in his eyes mirrored my own as he reached for my hand, his strong fingers wrapping around mine with a desperate tenderness.

"I don't know, Robin," he admitted, his voice thick with regret. "But I'll spend the rest of my life trying, if you'll let me."

Asa's unwavering devotion stirred something deep within me, a flicker of hope amidst the darkness of our shared sorrow. But could I trust him? Could I risk opening my heart again, knowing full well the dangers that lurked in the shadows?

I looked into his stormy gray eyes, searching for an answer, yet finding only a reflection of my own torment. I wanted desperately to believe in the promise of redemption, to embrace the possibility of a future together. But the chains of doubt held me captive, binding me to the past.

"Promise me," I whispered, my voice trembling with emotion. "Promise me that you'll fight for us, Asa. That you'll never give up, no matter how hard it gets."

He nodded solemnly, his gaze unwavering as he vowed, "I swear it, Robin. I'll fight for us until my dying breath.

We'll face the darkness together, and I won't let it tear us apart."

My heart ached with the weight of our unspoken fears, but in that moment, I allowed myself to entertain the faintest glimmer of hope. Perhaps, against all odds, forgiveness and redemption were still within reach. But only time would tell if our love could survive the shadows that threatened to consume us both.

A heavy silence settled between us, thick and oppressive as the shadows that danced along the walls. The flickering candlelight cast eerie patterns on Asa's face, highlighting the lines of his strong jaw and the shadows beneath his eyes. We sat there, side by side, our unspoken words hanging in the air like a phantom presence, adding to the tension and emotional weight of the scene.

Rain pattered softly against the windowpane, distant and disconnected from our world inside, a melancholy symphony played just for us. I stared at our intertwined fingers, feeling the warmth of his hand enveloping mine. But even in the midst of this fragile connection, my heart was burdened with doubt.

"Can I really forgive you, Asa?" I finally spoke, my voice barely above a whisper. "The loss...It's all-consuming. A gaping void where love and laughter once resided. And it's so hard to reconcile that with what I feel for you."

I saw his face fall, knew my words had wounded him, but I couldn't help it. His breath hitched, and I could see the pain etched across his features, a mirror to the turmoil raging within me. He swallowed hard, struggling to find the right words, his grip on my hand tightening ever so slightly.

"Robin, I understand," he said, his voice strained with emotion. "I would do anything, give everything I have, to take away your pain, to undo the damage I've caused. But I know that some wounds may never fully heal. All I can offer is my undying love and commitment, and the hope that, with time, we can rebuild what has been lost."

My heart ached, torn between the desire to surrender to his embrace and the nagging doubts about his true intentions. Could I trust him completely, knowing the dark secrets he harbored? Would the shadow of his past always cast its pall over our future?

"Time heals all wounds, they say," I murmured, a sad smile ghosting across my lips. "But what if the scars remain? What if they serve as a constant reminder of the pain we've endured?"

"Scars can't be erased," Asa admitted softly, his gray eyes searching mine intently. "But they can become a testament to our strength and resilience. A symbol of the battles we've fought and survived...together."

As his words resonated within me, I felt a flicker of hope ignite in the depths of my soul. A fragile flame, vulnerable to the winds of fate, but alive nonetheless. Only time would reveal whether forgiveness was possible, and if the love that bound us could withstand the trials that awaited us beyond the storm.

Asa's desperation weighed heavily in the room, his gaze never wavering from mine. "Robin, I swear to you, I'll do everything in my power to set things right. To atone for my past mistakes. Just tell me what you need from me, and I'll do it."

His words were genuine, but there was a part of me that hesitated, torn between forgiving him and protecting myself from any further heartache. I closed my eyes, attempting to drown out the torrent of emotions surging within me. The dimly lit room seemed to close in around us, as if bearing witness to the turmoil in my heart.

"Forgiveness isn't something I can just give away, Asa," I whispered, my voice trembling with the weight of my inner conflict. "I've been hurt too many times, and the thought of opening myself up to even more pain...I don't know if I can bear it."

"Please, Robin..." Asa's voice cracked, his eyes glistening with tears he wouldn't shed. "I understand your fear, and I would never ask you to take this leap blindly. But I promise you, all I want is to protect you, to love you, and to make amends for the pain I've caused. Let me show you that I'm not the man who brought darkness into your life. Let me be the one to stand by your side as we face whatever challenges come our way."

The vulnerability in his voice tugged at my heartstrings, making it difficult to maintain the walls I'd built around myself for protection. I could feel the pull of his sincerity, urging me to take a chance on him, despite my reservations.

"Trust me, Robin," Asa implored, reaching for my hand and holding it gently, yet firmly. "I won't let you down."

My breath hitched, and the scent of rain outside seemed to seep through the walls, mingling with the warm, flickering glow of candlelight. The distant patter of raindrops against the windows filled my ears, and I found myself swaying between two opposing forces: the ache for forgiveness and the fear of betrayal.

"Time...I need time," I finally said, my voice barely audible. "I can't promise you forgiveness, Asa. But I can try."

His shoulders sagged in relief, and he pulled me into his embrace, wrapping his strong arms around me as if I were a lifeline. As we stood there, enveloped in each other's presence, I allowed myself to consider the possibility of a future together, despite the dangers that still lurked in the shadows.

Raindrops streaked the frosted windowpanes, distorting the world outside. Asa's hand found mine, his fingers intertwining with mine as we braced ourselves for the conversation that would lay our souls bare. I wasn't sure I was ready for this, not after so much of my life had been little more than pain, suffering, and betrayal. But, for Asa? I'd try. I'd try very hard to bridge this gap forming between us. He was all I had left, and I wasn't willing to just throw that away, if it could be helped.

"Robin," he began, his voice quiet and uncertain, "I know I've hurt you. And I'm terrified that my past will only bring more pain into your life. But I need you to know...you mean everything to me. You're my whole world, and I never thought I'd know what love was, not after I lost my own family, not after Declan came and destroyed what little good there was left in me."

His words washed over me like a soothing balm, but they also stirred up the whirlwind of doubts in my heart. Could I really trust him? What if we were just setting ourselves up for an even greater fall?

"Everything we've gone through," I said softly, staring into the depths of his gray eyes, "it's hard not to question whether we're making the right decisions. We both know there are things we can't control, dangers that come with being close to you."

Asa swallowed hard, his Adam's apple bobbing in his throat. "I know. But I want to protect you, Robin. I'd give my life for yours if it came down to it."

The rain intensified outside, the droplets pelting the glass in a relentless rhythm that echoed my racing thoughts. Could we truly escape the darkness that seemed to follow us? Or would the ghosts of our pasts forever haunt us?

"Where do we go from here?" I asked, my voice wavering, as I searched his eyes for answers. "What if we can't outrun the danger that seems to be closing in on us?"

"Then we face it, Robin," Asa replied, determination etched on his face. "We can't change what's happened, but we can decide how we move forward. Together."

As our eyes locked, I realized that maybe, just maybe, forgiveness was possible. That despite the shadows that lingered in our pasts, we could carve out a future where love could exist alongside the pain. Maybe, just maybe, we could find healing together, somehow. I smiled faintly at that idea. Two ruined hearts healing each other, it sounded like something out of a poem, but it was what we were. What we are. Two ruined souls, reaching for each other in the darkness, looking to make a whole again. With each other.

"Alright," I murmured, squeezing his hand in reassurance. "We'll give it a try."

The corners of Asa's mouth lifted into a small, hopeful smile, and for the first time in what felt like an eternity, the darkness began to recede. And as the candlelight flickered, casting its warm glow over our faces, I saw a glimmer of hope, a fragile, beautiful spark that promised a future where love might heal even the deepest of wounds.

16

———

Robin

The crisp night embraced us as we strolled down the street, laughter spilling from our lips like the finest champagne, bubbles of joy in the dark. Asa's hand was warm in mine, his grip both gentle and unyielding. The tender sweep of his thumb over my knuckles felt like a promise, one I never knew I craved until him.

"You know, if a meal like that is what I get when you try to cook, I want you to cook more often." I teased, the smell of burned food still vivid in my memory, and probably within the house.

"Ah, I'm going to have to call it the infamous lasagna incident," Asa chuckled, his gray eyes twinkling with mischief beneath the moonlight. "I believe the fire department found it less amusing when the neighbors called them."

"Yet here we are," I mused, "alive and somehow not banned from all kitchen activities."

"Only because you saved the day...and the kitchen." His disarming smile widened. Despite the danger that clung to him like a shadow, he could still find humor in the little things. It was a gift, I supposed, or perhaps a necessity in his perilous world.

But as we turned a corner, drawing ever closer to the sanctuary of his house, unease threaded through my veins, weaving a web of doubt and desire that ensnared me. I knew the streets were watching, whispering secrets only Asa understood. The revelation that it had been he who sent Eamon after Angela lingered between us, an unspoken specter that refused to rest.

"Robin," he said, his voice low, as if he could sense the shift within me. "Whatever happens, you know I..."

"Shh," I interrupted, pressing a finger to his lips. "Don't. Let's just be us, for now." I couldn't bear to shatter the illusion of normalcy we'd crafted, even if it was built on a foundation of sand and secrets.

Asa's gaze searched mine, the intensity of his emotions laid bare in the dim light. In that moment, the man before me wasn't the enigma entangled with the Irish mafia; he was simply Asa, the one whose laughter melted into mine, whose touch set my skin ablaze with a longing I couldn't comprehend.

A woman like me, haunted by the specters of loss and betrayal, should've known better than to fall for someone like him. Yet, here I was, the skeptic who scoffed at love stories, suddenly cast as the leading lady in my own tumultuous romance.

It was madness, loving Asa Kelley, as unpredictable and treacherous as the sea during a storm. I should've wanted escape, to run far from the riptide that threatened to pull me under. But instead, I found myself diving deeper, reveling in the very thing I knew could drown me.

"Can't quit you, can I?" I whispered, more to myself than to him, as we paused before his door. My heart thundered against my ribcage, a caged bird desperate for the freedom I was unwilling to grant it.

"Never," he replied, his voice rough like gravel yet laced with a tenderness that unraveled me. "You're my unexpected forever, Robin Rodriguez."

His words, heavy with unspoken vows, hung in the air as he leaned in, his breath mingling with mine. The world faded away, leaving only the heat of his lips promising a forever I had never dared to imagine.

Laughter still lingered in the crisp night air, a remnant of our carefree moments, when the sharp crack of a board splintering against bone shattered the illusion of safety. Asa went down with a grunt, his towering frame crumpling like a marionette whose strings had been cut. I barely had time to register the shock in his gray eyes before rough hands gripped me, lifting me off my feet.

"Run, Robin!" Asa's voice was muffled, distorted by pain and the growing distance as I was dragged away, but it was too late. The world around me darkened, not from the night itself, but from a coarse bag that was thrust over my head, snatching away my vision and muffling my cries. Panic clawed at my throat, a wild thing desperate for release, yet there was no way out. It felt like the very breath was being stolen from my lungs.

The scent of oil and sweat permeated the fabric, invading my senses as I was heaved into what I assumed was a car. The engine roared to life, and we were moving, tearing through the streets that had once felt like the setting of a dream, our dream.

I tried to focus on the hum of the tires against the pavement, the slight shifts in acceleration and deceleration, anything to ground myself in this surreal nightmare. But my thoughts were a whirlpool, spinning between fear, confusion, and an inexplicable sense of betrayal. Hadn't I just admitted to myself that I loved this man? And now, here I was, ripped from his arms by violence and shadows.

Time lost meaning as we drove on, seconds stretching into eternities, each one more suffocating than the last. When the car finally stopped, and the doors opened, I was hauled out with a jarring lack of gentleness. My legs, numb from the ride, buckled beneath me, but my captors didn't falter. They carried me forward, their grip unyielding and impersonal.

A moment later, I was deposited onto a chair, the sudden contact with solid ground sending a shiver up my spine. There was a brief pause, a silence that buzzed in my ears louder than any scream could. Then, with a swift motion, the bag was torn from my head, bringing me face-to-face with reality once again.

Blinking against the harsh light, my gaze darted around, desperate to make sense of my surroundings. But all that greeted me was the cold stare of Eamon Doyle, his icy gaze piercing through me as though I were made of glass.

"Welcome, Miss Rodriguez," Eamon intoned, a cruel smile playing on his lips. "We have much to discuss."

And there, in that room stripped of warmth and hope, I realized that the dangerous world I couldn't abandon, the one I had chosen by loving Asa, had just claimed me as its own.

"Did you really think you could get away from me, Robin?" he sneered, his voice dripping with venom. His hand lashed out, smacking me harshly.

I swallowed hard, trying to ignore the sting of my split lip.

"You won't win, Eamon," I spat out, my voice trembling despite my best efforts to sound confident.

He laughed, a cruel, guttural sound that echoed through the empty streets. "Oh, sweetheart, I already have."

My thoughts raced as I searched for an escape, but there was none to be found. I felt trapped, cornered like an animal. The weight of the situation bore down on me, crushing my chest until it was difficult to breathe. My loved ones, they were all at risk because of me. Eamon and his ruthless Irish mafia would stop at nothing to destroy everything I held dear.

As Eamon continued to advance, I clenched my fists, refusing to back down. I knew I had to protect those I cared about, no matter the cost. This man, this monster, would not break me.

"Stay away from me!" I shouted, ignoring the pain that erupted in my face as I spoke. Eamon paused, momentarily taken aback by my defiance.

"Or what, Robin?" he challenged, a wicked smile stretching across his face. "What will you do?"

My mind raced, frantically searching for an answer. I knew that physically, I stood no chance against him. But there was something else, something deep within me, that refused to surrender. The memories of my mother and sister's deaths haunted me, their screams echoing through my mind like a never-ending nightmare. Their spirits urged me on, demanding justice for the injustice that had stolen them from me.

"Whatever it takes," I whispered, my voice barely audible over the pounding in my chest. "I will do whatever it takes to bring you down."

Eamon's smile faded, replaced by a cold, calculating expression.

"We'll see about that," he murmured, his voice low and menacing.

As he lunged toward me, I knew there was no turning back. This was it, the moment I had been both dreading and anticipating since I first crossed paths with Eamon Doyle. It would be either him or me; one of us would not walk away from this encounter.

Time seemed to slow as we collided, each of us fighting for our lives and what we believed in. My fear was eclipsed by the fierce determination burning within me, fueled by love and loss. As our struggle continued, I knew one thing for certain: I would not let Eamon win, not now, not ever.

The wind bit at my skin as I stumbled out of the alley, the taste of blood still on my lips. The violent encounter with Eamon left me shaken and desperate for solace. My heart raced, a reminder that those I cared about were still in danger. I needed Asa, his support and guidance more than ever before.

"Robin!" Asa's voice cut through the darkness like a beacon, pulling me towards him. He rushed to my side, his gray eyes filled with concern and worry. His strong arms enveloped me, offering warmth and protection from the merciless night.

"Tell me what happened," he urged, his breath ghosting over my ear as he held me close.

I recounted the chilling details of my confrontation with Eamon, feeling the tremor in my voice as the memories threatened to overwhelm me. Asa listened intently, his grip tightening with every word. When I finished, he pulled back slightly, just enough to look me in the eye.

"Robin, we're in this together," he said, his voice steady

and determined. "We'll take Eamon down and protect our families. I promise."

His words stirred something within me, a fragile sliver of hope that had been buried beneath the weight of my fears. But was it enough to carry me through the storm that lay ahead?

As we stood there, locked in each other's embrace, the demons of my past clawed at the edges of my mind. The memories of my mother and sister's deaths rose like specters, their lifeless faces haunting my thoughts. How many more lives would be shattered by Eamon's relentless pursuit of power? Would I ever be able to escape the darkness that seemed to follow me like a shadow?

"Robin," Asa whispered, drawing me back to the present. "Jim and Belinda are with me. We all came for you."

I allowed myself a moment to cling to the solace he offered, nestling my face against his chest and listening to the steady rhythm of his heart. His presence calmed my frayed nerves, soothing the torrent of emotions that threatened to consume me.

"Thank you, Asa," I murmured, my voice muffled by his shirt. "But I can't let others be hurt because of me. I have to face Declan and Eamon myself, no matter what it takes."

"You aren't doing it alone," he insisted, his voice filled with unwavering resolve. "We're stronger as a team, Robin."

"Alright," I agreed, lifting my head to meet Asa's gaze. "I know"

"I hope so," he replied, sealing his promise with a fierce kiss that left me breathless and aching for more.

The sky above us had darkened, its bruised hues a reflection of the storm brewing within me. Asa and I stood outside the bar where Belinda worked, the flickering neon sign casting ghostly shadows across our faces. The air was heavy with foreboding, as if it too shared my mounting dread.

"Belinda's in danger," I whispered, my voice barely audible above the wind's mournful wail. "Eamon's going after her next."

Asa's eyes narrowed, his jaw clenched in anger.

"We won't let him." His words were laced with a quiet fury that sent shivers down my spine.

I glanced around, searching for any sign of Eamon or his minions lurking in the shadows. The streets were deserted, save for the occasional stray cat skulking through the alleyways. But I knew better than to let my guard down; Eamon was a master of deception, forever plotting from the depths of the darkness that consumed him.

"Robin, we need to find her before he does," Asa urged, his hand gripping mine with a fierce determination that left my skin tingling with anticipation.

"Let's go inside," I suggested, pushing open the door with trembling fingers. The dimly lit interior of the bar was a comforting embrace, shielding us from the world outside.

"Belinda!" I called out, my voice cracking under the weight of my fear. "Where are you?"

"Over here, Robin," a timid voice replied, emerging from behind the bar like a frightened doe caught in the headlights. Belinda's brown eyes were wide with terror, her glossy black hair disheveled as if she had been running from an unseen threat.

"Is everything alright?" she asked, her gaze darting between Asa and me.

"Belinda, listen to me," I implored, grabbing her by the shoulders, feeling the frantic beat of her heart beneath my fingertips. "Eamon's coming for you. We need to get you out of here."

"Robin," Asa interjected, his voice soft yet firm. "We can't just run from him forever. We need to confront Eamon and put an end to this once and for all."

I studied his face in the dim light, searching for any trace of doubt or fear. But all I found was an unwavering resolve that mirrored my own. My heart ached with love and admiration for this man who had become my rock in this tempestuous sea of uncertainty.

"You're right," I conceded, swallowing the lump that had formed in my throat. "We can't keep running. It's time to face our demons."

"Are you sure?" Belinda asked, her voice barely audible above the pounding of my heart in my ears.

"More than ever," I replied, allowing a small smile to grace my lips as I embraced the growing certainty within me. "We'll take down Eamon and end this madness."

"Alright," Belinda agreed, her shoulders straightening as she squared up to the challenge before us. "I'm ready. Let's hunt that freak down."

As we prepared to leave the sanctuary of the bar, I couldn't help but be haunted by the ghosts of my past, my mother and sister, their lives cruelly snuffed out by the same darkness that now threatened to consume us all. But this time, things would be different. This time, I refused to let Eamon steal away those I held dear.

"Robin, I got some intel on Eamon's recent movements," whispered Asa, leaning over a worn table covered in maps and scribbled notes. The faint glow of a flickering light bulb illuminated his rugged face, casting shadows that accentuated his concern for our impending conflict.

"Good," I replied, my eyes scanning the information he had gathered. "We need every advantage we can get."

"Also, Marco said he could provide us with some

weapons." Belinda chimed in, her voice trembling despite the brave facade she wore. "I don't know how to use most of them, but I'll learn."

"Thanks, Belinda," I said, clapping a hand on her shoulder. "We'll need all hands on deck."

As I secured a pistol to my hip, Asa pressed a stiletto knife into my palm.

"For close encounters," he murmured, his gray eyes clouded with worry. A shiver crept down my spine as I gripped the cold steel, memories of past failures threatening to consume me.

"Will this be enough?" I wondered aloud, my voice barely a whisper. Doubt and vulnerability gnawed at my insides, each question a venomous bite eroding my resolve. "Can we really take on Eamon?"

"Robin," Asa said, his eyes locking onto mine, holding me steady amidst the storm of doubts swirling within me. "You are stronger than you know. We're here for you, and together, we will face him."

I nodded, swallowing hard against the lump of fear lodged in my throat. As I looked around at the determined faces of my allies, I felt a flicker of hope ignite within me, chasing away the shadows of despair.

"Alright," I whispered, steeling myself for the battle that lay ahead. "Let's do this."

We spent the remainder of the night strategizing and preparing, the darkness outside our refuge mirroring the uncertainty that weighed heavily upon us. As dawn broke over the horizon, casting a melancholic glow across the room, I knew that the hour of reckoning was fast approaching.

"Are you ready?" Asa asked, his hand gently squeezing mine as we stood on the precipice of our destiny.

"Ready as I'll ever be," I replied, my voice wavering only slightly as I met his gaze. My eyes brimmed with unshed tears, but I refused to let them fall – not now, not when there was still so much more to fight for.

"Remember," he murmured, his breath warm against my cheek, "no matter what happens, I will always be by your side."

"Thank you," I whispered, my heart swelling with gratitude and love for the man who had become my rock in this treacherous world. "I won't forget."

Together, we stepped out into the cold embrace of the morning, leaving behind the fragile sanctuary of our safe house, and ventured forth into the unknown.

The city streets were a labyrinth of shadows and secrets as I navigated my way through the maze, the weight of my newfound knowledge settling heavily upon my shoulders. I had spent hours poring over maps and intel, following leads that twisted and turned like the alleys I now traversed, but at last, I was closing in on Eamon's lair.

"Be careful," Asa whispered into the small earpiece tucked discreetly inside my ear, his voice a comforting anchor amidst the chaos. "He's a cunning one."

"Trust me, I know," I replied, my breath fogging the air as I peered around the corner, the chill of the early morning air seeping into my bones. "But he won't see me coming."

As I crept closer to my target, the knot in my stomach tightened, a coil of fear and anticipation wrapping itself around my heart. I couldn't shake the feeling that something was amiss, that Eamon was somehow watching me from the shadows, his eyes cold and calculating as he plotted my demise.

"Almost there," I murmured, my fingers brushing against the switchblade hidden within my coat pocket, my lifeline, the weapon Asa gave me for this deadly game of cat and mouse.

"Remember," Asa's voice crackled through the earpiece, his tone laced with concern, "don't hesitate. If it comes down to you or him..."

"I know," I interrupted, swallowing hard against the lump in my throat. "It won't be me."

As I approached the dilapidated warehouse that served as Eamon's stronghold, I could feel the tension in the air, thick and cloying as it constricted my chest and sent shivers down my spine. I knew that what awaited me inside would test the limits of my courage, but there was no turning back now.

"Showtime," I whispered, and with a deep breath, I stepped through the doorway.

"Ah, Robin," Eamon's voice slithered through the dimly lit space, echoing off the rusted metal walls. "I've been expecting you."

"Of course you have," I spat, my heart pounding in my chest as I searched for his elusive figure amongst the shadows. "You always were a coward, hiding behind others."

"Resourceful, not cowardly," he corrected, his mocking laughter sending a shudder of rage coursing through me. "But enough about me, let's talk about you. You've come so far, haven't you? From the frightened little girl who watched her family die to the vengeful woman standing before me now."

"Shut up!" I snarled, my grip on the pistol tightening as Eamon finally emerged from the darkness, his bald head gleaming beneath the flickering light. "This ends now."

"Does it?" he taunted, his icy gaze never leaving mine as we circled one another, predators locked in a deadly dance.

"You think you can defeat me, little bird? You're out of your depth."

"Maybe," I admitted, swallowing my fear as my resolve hardened, "but I'm not alone."

And with that, I fired at him, my bullet slicing through the air before it tore into his body and bones with a sickening crunch. He stepped back, his hand over the bleeding wound just below his shoulder. I wanted him dead. I wanted him dead right now so he could never hurt another woman again. I took aim again, this time, I aimed a little lower and a little more to the right.

"Give up, Robin," Eamon hissed, his fingers digging into his flesh as he tried to hold in the blood pouring out of the wound. "You can't win."

"Watch me," I spat, my arm out, the pistol steady in my grip. "This is for my family. This is for everyone you've hurt."

"Then do it already, if you're so fucking brave," he growled, his eyes narrowing as he prepared himself for my next shot.

As I pulled the trigger, my heart thundering in my chest, I knew that this was the moment of truth, the point of no return. It was now or never, and as the distance between us narrowed, I steeled myself for whatever outcome awaited me on the other side of this battle.

"Goodbye, Eamon," I whispered, and the world around us narrowed down to the bullet that raced into his heart. He dropped instantly with only a soft gasp as a protest.

"Checkmate," I whispered, holding the gun out, just in case he jumped back up.

But before I could put the gun away, before I could hunt down Asa and Belinda, a gunshot rang out, echoing through the warehouse like thunder. I felt a searing pain in my side, a white-hot agony that stole my breath and sent me staggering back.

I struggled to maintain consciousness, my thoughts spiraling into darkness as the implications of my actions weighed heavily on me. As blood pooled beneath me, the cold, unforgiving floor offering no comfort, I couldn't help but wonder: would Asa and Belinda ever truly be safe?

17

Robin

Blood seeped through my fingers as I pressed them to my side, my vision blurring with each ragged breath I took. I had been shot before, but it didn't make the pain any less excruciating. Declan's cold, merciless gaze lingered in my mind like a haunting specter, and I cursed myself for letting him get the upper hand.

Asa, Belinda, and Jim rushed to my aid, their frantic voices blending into a cacophony that echoed in my throbbing head. I tried to focus on Asa's reassuring words, but the world around me seemed to crumble as Declan emerged from the shadows once more. With a sinister grin, he aimed his gun at Belinda and pulled the trigger.

A gut-wrenching scream pierced the air, followed by a sickening thud as Belinda collapsed to the ground. Chaos erupted as Jim returned fire, the sharp crack of gunshots mingling with the acrid smell of burning gunpowder and blood.

"Robin! Stay with me!" Asa shouted, his voice a beacon

in the violence surrounding us. My heart raced as a primal fear coursed through my veins, urging me to flee for safety. But there was no escape from this nightmare, not while Belinda lay bleeding on the cold pavement.

The scene before me was a brutal dance of death; bullets tore through the air like ravenous wolves, seeking flesh to devour. The deafening roar of gunfire was punctuated by the anguished cries of the wounded, creating a symphony of suffering that filled my ears.

"Belinda," I whispered, the word escaping my lips like a prayer. Time seemed to slow as I watched her struggle for breath, her delicate features contorted in agony. A heavy weight settled in my chest as an overwhelming sense of helplessness consumed me.

"Focus on me, Robin," Asa urged, his gray eyes filled with a storm of emotions that mirrored my own. He reached for my hand, his touch a lifeline in the chaos that threatened to drown us both.

"Belinda..." My voice cracked with the weight of unshed tears, but I forced myself to meet Asa's gaze. "We can't...we can't let him get away with this."

Asa's jaw clenched, his resolve steeling within him.

"I promise you, Robin," he said, his voice thick with determination, "Declan won't escape justice. We'll make him pay for what he's done."

As my vision blurred from the pain radiating through my side, I struggled to focus on Belinda, her life slipping away before our eyes. Asa's hand tightened around mine, drawing me back to reality and solidifying our connection in the midst of the chaos.

"Stay with us, Belinda," Asa called out, his voice laced with both authority and desperation. Our shared concern for her fueled our determination to fight off the assailants, even as fear clawed at the edges of our minds.

"Cover me," I told Asa, my words coming out more like a plea than a command. My heart pounded wildly in my chest as I released his hand and moved towards Belinda, each step feeling like wading through a sea of shattered glass.

"Always," he replied, squeezing off a few rounds at the attackers, providing a momentary distraction.

I knelt beside Belinda, her breathing shallow and labored, her warm blood pooling around her like a crimson halo. Her brown eyes locked onto mine, pleading for help I wasn't sure I could give.

"Hold on, Belinda," I whispered, tears streaming down my face. "You're stronger than this. You can fight it."

"Robin..." She choked out my name, her grip on my hand weakening. A sense of urgency washed over me, and I knew we didn't have much time left.

"Dammit, we need an ambulance!" I shouted to Asa, my voice cracking under the strain of my emotions.

"Already called," he replied, his eyes never leaving our assailants. "Just keep talking to her, Robin. Keep her with us."

"Belinda, you promised me we'd dance until dawn, didn't you?" I asked, trying to evoke happier memories to keep her focused on staying alive. "We'll do that honey, once this is all over. I promise."

"Ro-Robin...I'm sor-sorry..." She gasped, her words barely audible as her body trembled with the effort of speaking.

"Shh, don't apologize," I urged, my heart aching at the sight of her suffering. "Just stay with us, please."

But as I watched the light slowly fade from her eyes, I knew there would be no more dances, no more laughter-filled nights. Grief threatened to swallow me whole as the cruel reality of Belinda's fate settled over me like a shroud.

"Robin..." Asa called out, his voice strained and hollow. "I...I think she's gone."

The sirens wailed in the distance, a cacophony of sound that did little to drown out my own anguished cries. Asa's arms wrapped around me like steel bands, holding me up as I sobbed over Belinda's lifeless body. The world swirled around us, a chaotic maelstrom of confusion and despair, but I barely noticed anything beyond my own pain.

"Robin, we have to go." Asa's voice was a low growl, his grief a palpable weight on his shoulders.

"Go?" I repeated numbly, my eyes still fixed on Belinda's face, her once-sparkling brown eyes now dull and empty. "How can we just leave her?"

"I don't want to do it either, baby, but we have to," he insisted, his grip tightening around me. "Declan knows we're here. We need to find a safe place and figure out what to do next. And you need time to heal."

"What comes next?" The word tasted bitter on my tongue, laced with grief and anger. My heart felt as if it had been carved from my chest, leaving me hollow and broken. "What could possibly come next after this? Belinda is... gone."

"Justice," Asa replied, his voice hardening with determination. "For Belinda, for your family, for everyone who has suffered at the hands of men like Eamon and Declan. We'll make them pay for what they've done."

"Justice..." I echoed, the concept both foreign and comforting. A flame ignited within me, fueled by rage and sorrow. As the paramedics arrived, carefully lifting Belinda onto a stretcher, I knew that our fight was far from over.

"Robin, I know it hurts," Asa whispered, his breath

warm against my ear as he tried to soothe me. "But you can't let this break you. You're stronger than that."

"Am I?" I questioned, my brain numb, my heart broken. "I couldn't save her, Asa. I couldn't save any of them."

"Maybe not," he conceded, his hand brushing against my cheek in a gentle caress. "But you can make sure their deaths weren't in vain. We'll bring down Declan together, Robin. For Belinda."

"Alright," I murmured, drawing strength from his words and the fierce resolve shining in his gray eyes. "For Belinda."

As we walked away from the scene, leaving behind the shattered remains of our once-peaceful evening, a single thought echoed through my mind, a vow that would guide my every action until justice was served:

Declan would pay. And I would be the one to make sure of it.

The sterile scent of the hospital hung heavy in the air, a constant reminder of the fragile line between life and death. Asa and I sat huddled together on a cold bench in the dimly lit hallway, our fingers intertwined as if clinging to one another would keep us from being swallowed by the darkness that threatened to consume us.

"Robin," Asa began hesitantly, his voice almost too soft over the hum of fluorescent lights above us. "You need to get your wound checked."

His eyes searched mine, piercing gray pools filled with concern and determination. A small, sad smile curved my lips as I squeezed his hand in response, grateful for the unwavering support he offered even in the face of such devastating loss. He'd known Belinda a lot longer than I had, but he was still trying to take care of me. I barely even felt the wound, though I wasn't sure it would stay that way. I looked at him, wishing I could make this go away, for all of us.

"It's a clean wound and the bullet exited about an inch from where it went in. I don't think it caught anything." I replied, though the wound ached painfully. It was nothing compared to the pain in my heart.

"I'd feel better if a doctor looked at it," he sighed, his hand on my face. I wanted to believe it was a gesture of comfort, but I have a feeling he was actually checking my temperature.

"Thank you, Asa," I murmured, my voice choked with emotion. "I don't know what I would do without you."

"Let's hope we never have to find out," he replied, the corners of his eyes crinkling as he attempted to lighten the mood. For a moment, I allowed myself to revel in the warmth of his presence, drawing strength from the conviction that radiated off him in waves.

"You'll see the doctor then," Asa asked, leaning in closer. His breath caressed my cheek, a welcome distraction from the chill that seemed to seep into my very bones.

I nodded, feeling the weight of responsibility settle heavily upon my shoulders. It was a burden I willingly bore, for Belinda and for all the others who had suffered at the hands of these monsters. My heart clenched painfully as I thought of her laughter, forever silenced by a bullet, a final memory I would carry with me until my own dying breath.

When I finally made it in to see the doctor, he checked the wound, put a stitch in it to make sure it stayed closed, but it had missed every vital organ it could have hit. I didn't think it was that bad, but the way the color came back into Asa face told me he hadn't thought so. Looking at my ruined shirt as I moved to put it back on, I could see why.

It was coated in blood. But was that all my blood or was some of it Belinda's too?

I sobbed and pushed the shirt away. Asa's brows pulled together, but then he looked down at the shirt and I saw realization dawning. He picked up the hospital gown I'd discarded and gave it back to me.

"Put this on, honey. It's...clean," he said, and the pained look in his eyes told me he understood well why I'd thrown my shirt in the floor. He picked it up now, held onto it, but then put it in the trash. For a moment, I almost protested, but then, I knew I'd never be able to look at it without horror and pain. Who wanted a memento like that?

"Where do we start?" I asked, my voice wavering with the enormity of the task before us.

"First, we need to let you heal," Asa replied, his eyes hardening with resolve. "Then, we need to find Declan's weak spots and exploit them. We'll dismantle his empire piece by piece until there's nothing left."

His plan held a certain poetic justice, and I couldn't help but imagine the satisfaction of watching Declan's world crumble around him as he was finally brought to his knees. It would never bring Belinda back, but it was a start, a chance to ensure that her sacrifice had not been in vain.

"That sounds like a plan," I breathed, feeling the fire within me reignite as I met Asa's steely gaze. "At least I took one of them down."

"You did," he answered, kissing me softly before he put his arms around me. "We have to wait, the police want a statement or something. But I'll get you home as soon as I can."

"I'm fine," I said and leaned against him.

We'd come to the hospital in the vain hope that Belinda was somehow still alive. That hope was now gone. Someone else I'd loved gone at the hands of a man so cruel he gave human life no value. Well, no life other than his own, that was. Tears stung my eyes all over again, not for Eamon, but for Belinda.

Jim was with the police, giving his statement, keeping them away from me. I would have to thank him for that later. Though the shadows of grief and uncertainty still clung to us like a shroud, one thing remained crystal clear: Declan's days were numbered, and we would be the ones to end them.

Hours later, I leaned against the cold metal railing of the hospital rooftop, gazing out at the city skyline as twilight settled in, a somber backdrop to our thoughts. Asa joined me, his gray eyes reflecting the melancholy that weighed heavily on both our hearts.

"Belinda would've been proud of you," he said softly, as if afraid to speak too loudly, as if he was afraid just his voice would shatter me entirely. And maybe he was right, maybe it would.

I nodded, my throat tight with emotion as tears threatened to escape. "She always believed we could take them down. Somehow, she knew we'd make it through all this darkness."

Asa's hand found mine, our fingers intertwining as we shared a quiet moment of reflection. Belinda had been our rock, our confidant, and our friend, his cousin. Her loss left an indelible mark on our souls. Yet, despite the pain, I could feel her strength within me, a guiding force urging us forward.

"Her memory will be our beacon through this storm," Asa murmured, squeezing my hand gently. "We'll honor her by finishing what we started, by bringing Declan to justice."

"Damn right we will," I agreed, a fire igniting within me

as I looked into his eyes, seeing the same determination mirrored there. "For Belinda, and for everyone else he's hurt."

In the fading light, the city seemed to shimmer with a dark promise, its shadows whispering secrets and taunting us with the dangers hidden within. Asa pulled me closer, wrapping his arm around my waist as we stared out at the city that held our past, our present, and our uncertain future. The wind picked up, tugging at our hair and clothes, carrying the echoes of Belinda's laughter and the memories of all we had lost.

"Get ready, Declan," I whispered into the night, a vow etched in steel and determination. "We're coming for you, and we won't stop until justice is served."

As we stood there, united by grief and purpose, a feeling of anticipation settled over us, a quiet calm before the storm. There was no turning back now. The stage was set for the final showdown, and it was time to bring it all crashing down.

18

Robin

The wind whispered through the trees outside the safehouse a few weeks later, a mournful melody that matched the heaviness in my chest. Asa's hand found mine as we stepped inside, his warmth providing a fleeting comfort against the chill of uncertainty.

"Everyone's here," he murmured, guiding me towards the small group assembled around a makeshift table. Jim stood with his arms crossed, eyes narrowed in thought, while our allies shifted nervously, occasionally casting furtive glances at one another.

"Alright, let's get started," I said, taking the lead as Asa squeezed my hand reassuringly. "We're here because we all have something in common. Declan O'Sullivan has hurt us in one way or another. We've gathered as much information as we could on his criminal activities, and now it's time to figure out how to bring him down."

"Here's what we know so far," Jim began, unfurling a map of New Orleans on the table, littered with red circles and scribbled notes. "Declan has his fingers in a lot of pies, but it's his control over the city's drug trade that gives him the most power."

"From what we've been able to gather, he has several key locations where he stores and distributes the drugs," Asa continued, tracing a line between the marked points on the map. "If we can take out these spots, we might be able to weaken his grip on the city."

"Sounds like a plan," I said, my determination fueling the fire within me. "But how do we do it without getting caught? He has eyes and ears everywhere."

"Maybe there's a way to use that against him," one of our allies suggested hesitantly. "He's got so many people working for him, it must be hard to keep track of everyone."

"True," I agreed, weighing the possibilities. "If we could blend in, infiltrate his organization without being detected, we might have a shot at gathering enough evidence to put him away for good."

"Or get ourselves killed," Asa countered, his gray eyes clouded with worry. "It's risky, Robin."

"Everything about this is risky," I reminded him gently. "But it's our best chance of finding justice for my family and everyone else he's hurt."

"Robin's right," Jim chimed in, his voice firm. "We can't let fear stop us from doing what's necessary."

"Then it's settled," I said, meeting each of their gazes in turn. "We'll find a way into Declan's criminal empire and expose him for the monster he truly is."

As we delved deeper into the details of our plan, a restless energy buzzed through the air, punctuated by whispered exchanges and the rustle of maps and documents. Our allies' faces were etched with determination and apprehension, mirroring the storm of emotions swirling within me.

In that moment, I knew that our lives would be forever changed by the path we had chosen. We were united by our shared grief and our resolve to bring Declan O'Sullivan down, no matter the cost.

I could feel the weight of the silence in the room, as heavy as the stagnant air that clung to my skin and threatened to suffocate me. My fingers traced the edge of the worn table, seeking solace in the familiarity of the rough texture beneath them. I glanced around at our small group of allies, their faces a mix of determination and fear. Jim's eyes met mine for a moment, offering a silent nod of encouragement.

"Alright," I began, drawing a deep breath to steady myself. "We need to gather hard evidence against Declan, something we can use to bring him down for good. I think our best shot is to infiltrate one of his secret meetings."

Asa leaned back in his chair, arms folded across his chest, gray eyes narrowed thoughtfully. "That's risky, Robin. If anyone recognizes us, we're as good as dead. We could confront him head-on instead, catch him off guard."

"Would he really be that careless?" I asked, my voice laced with doubt. "Declan's survived this long because he's always a step ahead. We can't afford any mistakes."

The taste of bile lingered at the back of my throat, a bitter reminder of the stakes we faced.

"Robin has a point," Jim interjected, his voice steady despite the tension that hung in the air like an unspoken plea. "Infiltration may be dangerous, but it offers us a chance to get close, learn his secrets and weaknesses. A direct confrontation might only serve to put us in even greater danger."

"True," Asa conceded, running a hand through his dark

hair. "But we need to consider the possibility that we might not make it out alive if we go undercover. Are we willing to risk everything for this?"

My heart hammered against my ribs, each beat a demand for justice, for retribution. I swallowed hard, banishing the tendrils of fear that threatened to choke me. "It's our best shot at putting an end to his reign of terror. We owe it to those who've suffered because of him, to my family. To Belinda."

"Robin's right," Jim agreed, his gaze unwavering. "We have a responsibility to see this through, no matter the cost."

Asa stared at me for a long moment, the conflict in his eyes reflecting my own turmoil. Finally, he sighed heavily and nodded. "Alright, infiltration it is. But we need to be prepared for anything. There's no telling what we'll find once we're inside."

Their words settled over me like a shroud, heavy with the knowledge of the danger we faced. And yet, as I looked into the faces of my allies, I sensed a flicker of hope amidst the uncertainty. I just hope it wasn't false hope.

A bead of sweat trickled down my temple, evidence of the tension that filled the dimly lit room. The flickering shadows cast by the single bare lightbulb above us felt like a physical manifestation of the uncertainty that weighed on all our minds. I couldn't help but admire the determined expressions on the faces of Jim and Asa.

"Alright," I said, breaking the silence as I wiped away the perspiration from my forehead with the back of my hand. "We need a compromise. One that won't put us directly in the line of fire, but still allows us to gather enough evidence to bring Declan down."

Asa's gray eyes met mine, a question lurking beneath the stormy depths. "What do you have in mind?"

"Instead of infiltrating his meeting or confronting him directly," I began, my voice steady despite the unease churning within me, "we gather evidence of his crimes, enough to expose him to the authorities and ensure his downfall without risking our lives in the process."

Jim rubbed his chin thoughtfully, his gaze lingering on the worn floorboards before returning to meet mine. "That might work, but it'd require meticulous planning and precision."

"I know," I admitted, feeling the weight of responsibility settle heavily upon my shoulders. "But it's our best chance at dismantling his empire while keeping ourselves out of immediate danger."

Asa studied me for a long moment, his eyes probing, searching for any trace of doubt within me. When he found none, he nodded slowly. "You're right. We have to be smart about this. If we can bring Declan down without putting ourselves in harm's way, it's worth the effort."

I let out a breath I didn't realize I'd been holding, relief flooding through me at his agreement. Still, I couldn't shake the sense of unease that gnawed at my insides, a reminder of the high stakes we faced.

"Robin," Asa murmured, his voice low and earnest, "I know how much this means to you, seeking justice for your family. I promise we'll do everything in our power to make sure Declan pays for his crimes."

The sincerity in his words stirred something within me, banishing the shadows of doubt that had threatened to take hold. I nodded, acknowledging the unspoken vow that bound us together in this desperate quest for retribution.

"Alright," I said, steeling myself for the challenges that lay ahead. "Let's get to work."

The house was dimly lit, its walls adorned with old

photographs and memories long forgotten. The smell of dampness filled the air, mingling with the faint scent of cigarette smoke that clung to our clothes. We huddled around a worn wooden table, a group of unlikely allies united by a common goal: to bring Declan O'Sullivan to justice.

"Alright," Asa began, his voice steady and commanding, "we need to devise a plan that gives us the best chance of success without putting anyone in unnecessary danger."

His eyes scanned the faces of each person present, gauging their resolve. I nodded, feeling the weight of expectation settle upon me like a heavy cloak. I knew my abilities would be crucial in this mission, but the thought of delving into Declan's dark secrets sent a shiver down my spine. Memories of my family's tragic past haunted me, casting shadows over my thoughts.

"Jim," Asa continued, addressing our burly ally who looked as if he'd been carved from stone, "you'll be our eyes and ears on the ground. Gather intel on Declan's movements and report back anything that might be useful to Robin."

"Got it," Jim grunted, his expression hard and unyielding.

"Marissa," Asa said softly, looking at the young woman who'd been Belinda's cousin until Declan killed her. She had a fire in her eyes that I recognized. I had that same fire within me. "You'll be responsible for keeping tabs on Declan's associates. Stay discreet, but gather any information you can about their activities and connections."

"Understood," she replied, determination etched into her features.

Asa turned back to me, his eyes warm and reassuring.

"We'll all work together, supporting each other every step of the way. We can do this."

"Thank you," I murmured, my voice barely audible. A knot of fear gnawed at my insides, but Asa's words bolstered my courage.

We spent hours refining our plan, discussing every detail and contingency until our minds were weary from the effort. The clock on the wall ticked away the minutes, its hands inching closer to the hour of our reckoning.

"Alright," Asa said finally, straightening up and rubbing his eyes, "I think we've covered everything. It's time to put our plan into action."

As we dispersed to our respective tasks, I retreated to a quiet corner of the house. I went back through the pages and pages of evidence I had on Declan and Eamon. But as I worked, the shadows of doubt that had plagued me since the beginning of our mission continued to whisper their insidious warnings. Was I strong enough to confront the darkness that awaited me? Could I truly trust the people who now stood by my side?

With each passing moment, the stakes grew higher, the danger more palpable. Yet, despite the uncertainty and unease, I was determined to press forward, fueled by a burning desire for revenge that would not be quenched until Declan O'Sullivan paid for his sins.

The steady hum of the city outside was a constant reminder that life went on, oblivious to the dangerous game we were playing. It seemed almost unreal, the contrast between the ordinary world out there and the precarious balance of trust and betrayal we were navigating within the safehouse's walls.

"This is it," Asa said, his voice low and serious as he and Jim prepared to leave for their mission, "we'll need every scrap of intel we can find about Declan's operations. The more we learn, the better our chances of taking him down."

Jim nodded, his graying hair catching the dim light that seeped through the drawn curtains. "I've got a few contacts I can reach out to, people who owe me favors. They might be willing to share some information."

"Good," Asa replied, clasping Jim's shoulder in a gesture of solidarity. "And I'll do the same with my connections. We've got to expose any vulnerabilities in Declan's organization that we can exploit."

As they readied themselves to step into the underworld that had once consumed them, I couldn't help but feel the weight of the risk they were taking on my behalf. Their actions would place them squarely in Declan's crosshairs, and the thought sent an icy shiver down my spine.

"Be careful, both of you," I implored, my heart heavy with concern. "I don't want anything to happen to either of you because of me."

Asa turned to me, his gray eyes piercing through the shadows that hung over us. "We're in this together, Robin. And we won't stop until we've brought Declan to justice."

"Besides," Jim added with a wry smile, "it's not just for you. It's for Belinda. And it's about time someone put an end to his reign of terror."

"Right," Asa agreed, before turning to address the rest of our gathered allies. "Mick, you'll be in charge of creating a diversion while we're gathering intel. Keep their attention focused away from our activities."

"Understood," Mick replied, his eyes narrowing in determination. "I'll do whatever it takes to throw them off your trail."

As Asa and Jim slipped out into the night, I was left with my own role in our plan, find more dirt on him. I wasn't sure

I'd find anything in Declan's files but I hoped I would unearth something new, evidence that would seal his fate. My fingers trembled slightly as I laid them on the paper, the weight of our mission pressing down on me like a suffocating fog.

I took a deep breath, pushing aside the whirlwind of emotions that threatened to engulf me, fear, doubt, longing. Instead, I focused on the task at hand, knowing that I had to be strong for those who had risked everything in pursuit of justice. As my fingers began to dance across the pages, I steeled myself for the challenges ahead, determined to see our mission through to its end, no matter what perils we faced or sacrifices we made.

"Be safe," I whispered into the darkness, a silent plea to Asa and Jim as they ventured deeper into the heart of danger. And with each click and clack of the keys, I vowed to honor their courage by doing everything in my power to ensure that we would succeed.

The clock on the wall ticked away, each second feeling like an eternity as I sat around the table in Asa's house. Shadows danced on the faces of Asa, Jim, and our small group of trusted allies, their tension gone, and all of them were more relaxed. Somehow, they'd managed to break into Declan's main office undetected and steal a load of files. I could only guess he thought he'd dealt us a blow that would keep us in check, and he'd relaxed a little too much. He shouldn't have done that.

"Anything useful," Asa said, his voice low and steady. "If any of you find anything, anything at all that seems unusual, bring it up."

Jim nodded in agreement, his tired eyes scanning the files and folders scattered before us. "I haven't found anything yet, but that doesn't mean I won't. Anybody else?"

I chewed my lip, considering the complexities of the task at hand. "I have a few things, but nothing that bring the feds down on him, so far."

"There has to be something in here," Asa's gray eyes met mine, concern mingling with determination. "There has to be."

"Agreed," Jim added, his gaze flickering between Asa and me.

"We'll keep looking," I chimed in, my stomach twisting with anxiety. "If Declan figures out it was us that stole his files, it's game over for all of us."

A somber silence settled over the room as we acknowledged the gravity of our situation. Each of us knew that the consequences of failure could be dire.

"Let's make sure we don't fail," Asa declared, his voice tinged with steel. "We've all got our roles to play, and I know that each of us will give it everything we've got."

"Damn right," Jim muttered, his jaw clenched in determination.

As we finalized the details of our plan, the shadows around us seemed to grow darker, whispering of the dangers that lurked just beyond our reach. But amid the uncertainty and unease, one thing remained clear: we were united in our cause, bound together by a shared desire for justice.

"We can do this," I repeated, my voice barely audible above the ticking of the clock. "And then, hopefully, we'll have the evidence we need to bring Declan down, and finally put an end to this nightmare."

A quiet chorus of agreement followed, our resolve solidifying like iron in the forge of adversity. We knew the risks we were taking, the potential consequences of our actions. But there was no turning back now. Our path had been set, and all that remained was to see it through.

The air in the house was heavy with tension, the weight of our shared fears and uncertainties pressing down upon us. I stared into the flickering flames of a solitary candle, its wavering light casting eerie shadows on the walls. The scent of burning wax mingled with the aroma of stale cigarettes and whiskey, creating an oppressive atmosphere that seemed to choke the very life from me.

"Find it," I whispered to myself, as if saying it aloud would give the words a certain power, a sense of reality that made them more than just a figment of my desperate imagination. "Find the evidence and then we'll know if this was all worth it."

Asa looked at me, his piercing gray eyes searching my face for any sign of doubt or hesitation.

"Robin, are you sure you're alright?" he asked, his voice tinged with a gentle concern that belied his rough exterior.

I met his gaze, feeling the warmth of his presence like a balm against the chill that had settled in my bones.

"Yes," I replied, my voice steadier than I'd expected. "I have to be. This is our chance, maybe our only chance, to bring Declan down and get justice for Angela...for Mom and Belinda."

A soft murmur of agreement rippled through the room, each of us bound by the same grim determination. We knew the risks, the dangers that lay ahead. But the fire that burned within us, could not be extinguished by fear alone. I felt a strange sense of peace wash over me. We were walking a razor's edge, teetering between life and death, hope and despair. But we would not falter, nor would we give in to the fear that gnawed at our hearts.

THE SCENT of cleaner hung heavy in the air as I meticulously cleaned my pistol, each movement deliberate and precise. The dim light from the solitary bulb above glinted off the cold metal, casting odd shadows on the walls of the safehouse. Asa and Jim were hunched over a stack of papers nearby, their murmured conversation punctuated by an occasional grunt or curse.

"Keep your mind sharp and your aim sharper," my uncle's words echoed through my thoughts, an old mantra that had been engrained in me since childhood. It was a familiar comfort, a tether to the past that helped steady my nerves as the reality of our plan began to sink in.

"I will," I whispered to myself, feeling both exhilaration and trepidation at the thought.

"Everything alright?" Asa asked, his voice soft but laced with concern as he approached. His gray eyes searched mine for any sign of doubt or hesitation, but I refused to let my vulnerability show.

"Fine," I replied tersely, swallowing the lump in my throat. "Just...preparing."

He nodded in understanding, his fingers brushing against mine as he handed me a fresh clip of ammunition. The electric warmth of his touch sent a shiver down my spine, and for a fleeting moment, I allowed myself to imagine a life beyond this mission, a life with Asa by my side. I'd never imagined such a thing with any other man before. None of them seemed worth the time. But Asa did.

"Stay focused, Robin," I reminded myself, shaking away the daydream. There would be time for such fantasies later, if we survived.

"Asa," I called out, shifting my attention back to the task

at hand. "What can you tell us about the layout of Declan's compound? We need to know every entrance, exit, and possible hiding place."

"Working on it," he grumbled in response, scratching his stubble as he scrutinized a crudely-drawn map. "Best I can do without getting inside, but it should give us a decent idea of what we're up against."

"Better than nothing," Jim muttered, his expression grim with determination. "We'll make do."

"Make do" seemed to be the motto of our ragtag alliance.

I steeled my nerves as I slid the ammunition into my pistol with a satisfying click. I looked up to find Asa watching me closely, his gray eyes filled with a mixture of fear and admiration. He understood the risks we faced, the sacrifices we were willing to make for our cause, and yet, he still chose to stand by my side.

"You're beautiful," he whispered softly, his hand coming to rest gently on my shoulder. The warmth of his touch seeped through the fabric of my shirt, a physical manifestation of the unwavering support that had become the foundation of our alliance.

"If you say so," I added, my voice barely audible as I stared down at the weapon in my hands. It was a symbol of both our strength and our vulnerability, a reminder that our lives hung in the balance.

"I insist, you are," Asa said, his words a solemn vow that resonated deep within my soul. With our plan in place, it was time to prepare for the mission ahead, mentally, physically, and emotionally. And as the weight of responsibility settled heavily on my shoulders, I took solace in the knowledge that I would not face this darkness alone.

19

______

Robin

The low hum of the refrigerator was a mocking reminder of our scant provisions. I leaned against the kitchen counter, staring blankly at the empty shelves. Asa's presence loomed behind me, his heat a comforting contrast to the cold stainless steel.

"We're out of groceries," I murmured, lost in thought as my fingers traced the worn pattern on the laminate surface.

"Robin," Asa's voice, deep and smooth, pulled me from my reverie. "I'll head out and get what we need."

His hand found its way to my shoulder, a gesture of familiarity and comfort.

"Are you sure?" I asked, my gaze lifting to meet his gray eyes. They held a storm of things unsaid, swirling with concerns he tried to keep from me.

"Absolutely," he assured me, his thumb brushing against my jaw in a tender caress. "You'll be safe here."

Once Asa stepped out, the silence of the house settled around me like an old, familiar blanket, woven through with threads of solitude. I pondered over dinner plans, the clatter of pots and pans an aimless symphony accompanying my thoughts. Perhaps he'd bring back some steak and I could make a hearty stew, or maybe his favorite, spaghetti carbonara.

The decision still fluttered in my mind when the front door surrendered to a violent kick, shattering the illusion of safety. My heart seized in terror, adrenaline surging as shadowy figures spilled into the once tranquil space. Instinctively, I backed away, but my retreat was cut short by the kitchen island.

"Get her!" one of them barked, his voice slicing through the chaos.

Panic clawed up my throat, and I fought, lashing out wildly, my hands finding flesh, fabric, anything. Their hands were everywhere, grasping, pulling, restraining. A scream tore from my lungs, a desperate, primal sound that echoed off the walls, pleading for Asa, for anyone, to help me. I'd forgotten about my gun, tucked under my jeans and inside my cowboy boots, and now that the men were on me, I couldn't get to it.

"Quiet down!" The command was punctuated by a fist colliding with my cheek, and the world tilted dangerously. Pain exploded across my face, radiating out in sharp tendrils as my vision blurred and doubled.

"Please," I gasped, the fight draining from me as quickly as it had come. But the darkness on the edge of my consciousness was relentless, creeping closer with each ragged breath I took.

There was a moment, brief and surreal, where the mayhem seemed to slow, the air thick with the coppery tang of fear. I could almost taste the lingering remnants of Asa's last kiss. Would he find me?

And then, nothingness embraced me, and I succumbed to its cold, unwelcome arms.

Consciousness returned to me like the slow, torturous drip of a leaking faucet. Each drop of awareness was cold and jarring against the backdrop of my throbbing head. My eyelids fluttered open, revealing the dimly lit expanse of Declan's main warehouse office, a cavernous room steeped in shadows and terrible secrets.

I lay there for a moment, disoriented, the taste of copper and fear lingering on my tongue. The scent of sawdust and motor oil hung heavy in the air, mingling with the more subtle undercurrents of old leather and tobacco, a signature blend that belonged unmistakably to this place, to *him*.

Relief surged through me when I remembered the weight pressed against my calf; the small, lethal comfort nestled inside my cowboy boots. With painstaking care, I shifted, my fingers slipping into the worn leather to wrap around the cool metal of my concealed gun. A silent prayer of thanks escaped my lips for the foresight that had prompted me to arm myself this way.

The gun was a quiet promise of potential power as I slid it out and positioned it behind my back. My heart pounded a frantic rhythm against my rib cage, the sound deafening in the stillness. I was a caged bird, wings clipped but talons sharp, waiting for the moment to strike.

It didn't take long for Declan to make his entrance, the door swinging open with an authoritative push that seemed to roll through the warehouse like thunder. He strode in with the confidence of a man who believed the world owed him its allegiance, his dark hair sprayed to within an inch of its life.

"Ah, Robin, awake at last," he crooned, his voice dripping with a venomous satisfaction that made my blood run cold. "You know, I've always considered Asa my own personal toy. It's a game, you see, watching him squirm, thinking he's got any semblance of control."

I remained silent, keeping my breathing even, though each word he uttered stoked the fires of my rage, the flames licking at the edges of my composure. His presence filled the room, oppressive and thick, and I could feel the heat of his gaze as he circled me like a shark scenting blood in the water.

"He never learns, does he?" Declan continued, a chuckle lacing his words. "Always playing the hero, so strong, so sure. But we both know it's an act, don't we? Beneath that muscular facade lies nothing but weakness and vulnerability."

The disdain in his tone was palpable, a living thing that coiled around my resolve and tried to squeeze the life from it. I fought the urge to recoil, to let the terror that gnawed at my insides show. Instead, I focused on the steel within me, the icy determination that whispered of survival and retribution.

Declan stopped just before me, his shadow falling over my face like the shroud of the reaper. He leaned in close, his breath hot against my skin, and I knew this was the moment. My hand tightened around the gun, my resolve crystallizing into an unbreakable shard of purpose.

"Are you ready to play, Robin?" he asked, his voice a low growl that resonated with dark promises.

"Always," I replied, though the words were a mere thought, lost amidst the clamor of my racing heart. The gun was hidden, pressed against my spine, and I prayed for the strength to use it when the time came. I felt the cold press of the gun against my back, a secret shard of defiance in a room that reeked of power and corruption.

"Robin," Declan murmured, circling me like a predator sizing up its prey. "There's something familiar about you."

His voice was velvet draped over iron, soft yet unyielding. He was close now, too close, his presence a suffocating heat against the chill of fear that crawled beneath my flesh.

"Is that so?" I managed, my voice betraying none of the turmoil that raged within. My heart was a frantic drummer, setting a violent tempo for the dread and anticipation that played out in the caverns of my chest.

He leaned in, and I felt the brush of his breath against my ear. There was a hunger in it, primal and unsettling.

"Mmm," he hummed, his tone dripping with an arousal that made my skin crawl. "You remind me of someone...someone I can't quite place."

It was then, with his lust clouding his judgment, that I seized my moment. Swift as a snake, my hand moved from behind my back, the gun now a cold extension of my will. I pressed the barrel firmly against his ribs, right where his heart, a blackened thing, no doubt, would be caged within.

"Maybe this will jog your memory," I whispered, my voice a ghostly echo of the sister he had torn from this world. "I remind you of Angela. The sister you murdered without a second thought."

Declan's eyes widened, a flicker of realization igniting in their depths before the shadows reclaimed them. It was the look of a man staring down the abyss, finding it gazing hungrily back at him.

"Angela...," he breathed, the syllables a curse upon his lips.

"Yes," I confirmed, the word a bullet itself, loaded with all the sorrow and rage that had festered in my soul since her laughter had been stolen from the world.

And with a heart heavy as stone, but with a spirit

unyielding as the tide, I pulled the trigger. The sound tore through the silence, a thunderclap that spoke of finalities and endings. It was the punctuation mark at the end of a long, tragic sentence, a period inked in blood and vengeance.

As the echo of the gunshot faded to a whisper, I stood alone amidst the ruins of justice and sin, the taste of retribution bitter on my tongue, the weight of my choices a shroud upon my shoulders.

For a moment, I stood frozen, staring at the man who had been both my tormentor and an enigma. My breath came in ragged sobs, the aftermath of adrenaline leaving me as unsteady as a leaf in the hurricane's wake.

"Goodbye, Declan," I whispered, the words a funeral dirge for all that had been lost.

And then, there was nothing but the sound of my heartbeat, the proof that I was alive, and he was not. I ran past his still body and out of his office. The warehouse was a labyrinth of shadows and sorrow, a place where the ghosts of my past seemed to clutch at my heels with every step. My heart drummed a frantic rhythm against my ribcage as I navigated through the dim corridors, the metallic tang of blood still clinging to my hair. Declan's lifeless form was etched into my retinas, an unyielding reminder of what I had done.

I stumbled forward, propelled by fear and determination, my gun a cold comfort in my trembling hand. The clamor of New Orleans' streets felt worlds away, muffled by the thick walls that imprisoned me. I had to escape, to emerge from this tomb of concrete and steel before the darkness consumed me entirely.

As I rounded a corner, a faint sound cut through the silence, a chorus of muffled cries, like a lament carried on the wind. My pulse quickened. This wasn't just about my own freedom anymore; there were others who needed salvation. Pushing aside a heavy curtain, I moved toward the source.

There it was, an 18-wheeler, its vastness swallowing the space. This must be the shipment Declan's been waiting on, I thought, spurred on to open the doors when I heard the human sounds coming from within. The whispers and moans grew louder, a sign of desperation that the people inside couldn't hide. I reached out a shaking hand and pulled the door fully open.

Inside, a sea of faces met my gaze, women with eyes that reflected stories of stolen dreams and fractured hopes. They were the mysterious shipment, the human cargo whispered about in hushed tones along the French Quarter, their lives to be bartered like trinkets in Declan's twisted marketplace.

One woman confronted me, her voice fragile uncertainty. Were they free? I didn't have to understand her language to understand that question. I waved behind me and the women began to move.

"You're free, go" I assured her uncertain what her language was. I had a suspicion they may be Vietnamese, based on our recent escapades in that country. Declan may have bought them there, with a plan to sell them here, but I'd just put an end to all of that. I gestured again to get the women moving faster.

"Free," I said in English, more firmly. "He's gone. You're free."

Their release was almost a bandage over the raw wounds etched upon my heart, a flicker of light in the overwhelming gloom. Almost. I'd lost my sister and mother, we'd all lost Belinda, but these women had their own lives back. As I led them out of the truck, each uncertain step they took was a testament to resilience, a mirror of my own journey through the abyss.

In freeing them, I found hope that I could get on with my life. But first, I needed to find my way back to Asa, to slip through the fingers of a city that had seen too much. With every breath, I carried the weight of their liberation, a burden made lighter by the knowledge that we were all escaping together, away from the grasp of a man who no longer held dominion over any of us.

The pier loomed ahead, a beacon of hope amid the encroaching darkness. We moved as a collective, an exodus born from the ashes of tragedy. And somewhere within me, a resolve solidified: I would never stop running until the dawn greeted us all with the promise of a new beginning.

I stumbled forward, my breath jagged as it escaped in short bursts, the warm air hot in my lungs. My limbs were heavy, each step weighted with the gravity of what had happened to all of us. The scent of salt and rust clung to the night, a tangy reminder of bloodshed and the sea. I had left the warehouse far behind, the moon's ghostly luminescence guiding me through the labyrinth of New Orleans' docks.

The echo of my footsteps bounced off the silent containers, a rhythmic heartbeat in the stillness. The taste of freedom was bittersweet on my tongue. For every inch of ground I gained, memories clawed at my heels, Belinda's laughter turned into deathly silence, her vibrant life snuffed out by Declan's merciless hand. Now he was among the dead, another man I had killed. Another man that had deserved it.

Then, through the haze of fatigue and fear, a figure emerged, solid and real against the backdrop of uncertainty. Asa. His presence cut through the night like a beacon, his compelling gray eyes locked onto mine with an intensity that grounded me to the spot. "Asa."

"Robin," he breathed, his voice a lifeline thrown amidst the tempest of my emotions.

With steps that felt like they were encased in mud, I moved toward him, my heart hammering against the walls of its cage. The closer I got, the more pronounced the tremors racking my body became, until they culminated in a quake that threatened to tear me apart. As if sensing my imminent collapse, Asa stepped forward, arms open and ready to catch the fragments of my being.

The moment his arms closed around me, the dam broke. Every pent-up emotion, every shard of pain and flicker of fear, it all unraveled in the sanctuary of his embrace. My knees buckled beneath me, as I told him what had happened. I finally surrendered to the exhaustion that washed over me like a relentless tide. I collapsed against him, my head resting against the solid warmth of his chest, the steady beat of his heart a contrast to the chaos of mine.

"You're safe now, darlin'. Safe," he murmured, a vow woven into the word, wrapping me in a shroud of protection I hadn't known I craved. His scent enveloped me, a mix of leather and something indefinably Asa, a fragrance that spoke of danger and comfort in equal amounts. "God, I love you so much."

"I love you too, Asa. Please, stay. Stay with me," I whispered, the plea wrapped in desperation and hope. There was no strength left within me to stand alone, not when the world seemed intent on swallowing me whole.

"Always," he promised, his voice a rumble against my ear, a sound that resonated within me.

As we stood there, locked in an embrace that was both an end and a beginning, I allowed myself to believe, for just a moment, in the possibility of escape, not just from the physical chains of the past, but from the shadows that lingered within. With Asa's arms around me, perhaps the dawn could bring more than just the light. Perhaps it could bring healing, too.

Thank you for reading my book. If you liked this story, I think you'll enjoy my FREE book **Mafia's Dirty Secret**. Here's an exclusive sneak peek for your eyes only.

MARIE RAN the warm washcloth down her mother's rigid arm. The tremors were worse today, she noted as she washed the soap from her mother's skin. The washcloth moved down to the tips of the woman's fingers, and Marie noted for the millionth time that her mother still had slim, shapely fingers.

She dipped the cloth in the pink, plastic basin that had come from... somewhere. The hospital on her mother's last visit, that was where they got it, she remembered now. She brushed black, silky strands of her hair from her naturally tan face with the back of her hand and looked away from her mother. It was too hot to work like this, but she couldn't afford anyone else to help her.

A tear slid down her face, but she swiped it away angrily. Self-pity wasn't something she'd often allowed herself to wallow in, but sometimes it was hard not to. Her mother had lost all ability to care for herself, and it was now down to Marie to do it for her.

"Mar-..." came her mother's garbled voice. Sometimes the woman could barely speak, and at others, her voice was clearer. Marie brushed short, white hair from her mother's face. A face that had once been on movie posters, with shiny dark-brown hair and sassy eyes was now little more than a shell of what used to be. All that French and Spanish heritage had melted with time, into the face of a woman old before her time.

"I know, Mom, I'm trying to hurry." Marie moved to the other side of her mother's hospital bed, made sure the blue plastic pads with an absorbent center protected the sheets, and began to wash her mother's other side. Then she'd work on the middle, her back, and finally, her legs and feet.

It was a process she'd learned from the home health agency that paid her wages. As her mother's own Personal Care Assistant, she was paid to do the tasks Ruby wouldn't have allowed someone else to do. It allowed Marie to have an income, take care of her mother, and kept them both fed. A state agency paid for it all, some program or another that Marie had signed her mother up for a long time ago. That was back when she first had to use a wheelchair and could get out of bed.

Back when Marie had been on her way to Louisiana State University with dreams in her head and hope in her heart. Now, she was her mother's slave, the same as always. At least now she didn't have to be verbally abused too. Her mother could barely speak, even when she was lucid, and that kept her sharp tongue in check.

Marie felt terrible for the thought and winced as she promised she'd do penance later. For now, she had to wash her mother's torso, then the rest. She always tried to think of something else as she went through the task she'd been trained to do. She'd think of the beach she wanted to go to, or the restaurants not far away. She'd think about what she'd order from the menu, and what she would do once she had her toes in the sand.

Marie left the small room with blacked-out windows. They'd done that to protect her mother's eyes. She'd claimed the light hurt, but Marie had often wondered if it was to keep the world at bay. If she couldn't see out, nobody could see in. It had always been that way. All of her life, Ruby hid them both from the world, from outsiders as she'd called them.

Once she was done with her mother's torso, the young woman walked into the bathroom just opposite the bedroom her mother had claimed and rinsed out the tub. As she filled it with warm, clean water, Marie hummed to herself, a song she'd heard on the radio. Cajun music was her favorite, and she often left the radio playing, even when she went to sleep.

"Unwan...," Ruby groaned as Marie came in.

Marie sighed, but let it go. "Unwanted bitch", that's what her mother was trying to say. Even now, when Marie did all she could to keep her clean, free from bedsores, and in clean clothes, her mother was cruel.

She always had been though.

Marie had always known that she wasn't wanted. She could remember her mother saying it when she was two years old, then three, then every year after. Even when

Marie was 18 and ready to leave her mother, at long last, her mother had said it. She'd spit it that day, but she'd added a new twist.

Ungrateful.

Marie was ungrateful for the long, miserable life her mother gave her. That's how she'd announced the news that she was sick, she'd called Marie an ungrateful, unwanted bitch that wouldn't even stick around to take care of her sick mother. Marie had only wanted to escape the torment, but she'd cracked and stayed.

Her mother's Parkinson's had progressed enough that the doctors had finally stopped blaming the car accident that had killed Marie's father and nearly took her mother's life. They'd done round after round of tests and finally concluded that the tremors, the loss of balance, and the rigidity in her mother's left arm was from Parkinson's disease. It was at an advanced stage by then, and Marie was as doomed as her mother.

Doomed to always be there for her.

Marie felt guilt over her quiet anger, her resentment of her mother. She knew she should have been a better daughter, that she should try harder for her mother, but some days, like today, the resentment got the better of her. It was hot, sticky hot, and flies were buzzing around already. The mosquitos would come later, breaking through the mosquito nets to leave her with itchy welts.

She wanted out of this place, to be somewhere where she could afford air conditioning, where someone else took care of her mother. Where she wasn't a slave to a woman that had hated her for her very existence.

"You were supposed to be aborted, that's what your father wanted. But we had the accident, and here you are, all mouth and selfish." She could remember her mother saying that to her when she was five and needed new shoes because she'd outgrown the old ones.

Marie had learned to just make do with what she had until her mother noticed her clothes didn't fit, or the school called her to threaten they'd report her if she didn't take better care of her little girl. Those days had been the worst because Marie would come home to a raging, hateful mother that pulled at her arms until it left bruises as she dragged her daughter out to the car, into a store, and threw her down to try on clothes or shoes. Or bras.

She shuddered as she remembered the first time her mother took her to shop for bras. There'd been hisses about how her daughter wouldn't turn out to be a little slut and no she couldn't have the soft, lacy bras that were comfortable; she'd wear this plain cotton contraption that was so tight it left lines around her ribcage.

Her mother wasn't the sweet and loving angel so many other kids around her had. Not at all.

Marie scrubbed at her mother's back, checked her skin while she dried it for signs that she might be getting bedsores, and moisturized the skin. She picked up another washcloth, a clean one, and then she tackled her mother's privates, a job she hated to do. It felt like she was doing something wrong. She knew it needed to be done, that her mother had to be clean everywhere, but damn if it didn't feel like an invasion.

She hummed another song as she slid the cloth down around the necessary parts, her brain frozen, no thoughts entered at all, as she pulled the cloth out, rinsed it, then rinsed the soap away. More clean water. She'd have to do the laundry today, get it hung out on a line, and then brought back in. When she got back from the grocery store, she'd take it all down and fold it up.

She was nearly done now, only her legs and feet. Marie inspected her mother's heels, the back of her calves and thighs, any pressure points, and decided to put on the special boots the doctor gave her to protect her mother's feet. They kept the heels off the bed, and suspended so there would be no pressure, and thus, no sores.

She checked her mother's elbows one more time, and finally took the tub away. She cleaned the blue tub with hot water and put it on a rack to dry. She'd need it again in the evening. Or if her mother had an accident. It happened sometimes, and Marie would have to wash her up again if it did.

Her mother wasn't gone, mentally, it was just physical, her mother's problem. Sometimes she would hallucinate or show signs of dementia, but it wasn't often. Not yet, anyway. Marie knew what the future held as her mother's disease progressed and was ready for it. She hoped.

She went into the kitchen and sat down at the table to rest. It was topped with cheap plastic, with wood particles coming free from the edges. It was probably older than Ruby herself, but it was all they could afford now. Once the house hadn't looked so bad, Marie knew. Her mother had made a little money from the film she made, and every now and then, she'd still get a royalty check. Not often, but every now and then.

It had been enough, back then, to buy the five-bedroom house with two bathrooms, and two floors. Most of the rooms were empty now, and the doors stayed closed. In the winter it was too hard to warm rooms that were never used anyway. She'd sold the items inside the rooms, to pay for her mother's care, and to pay the bills. Now, her mother had a disability check, and government medical insurance, but it didn't pay for everything.

At least Marie was getting paid to take care of her. If she'd had to do it without pay, she might have lost her mind as she struggled to pay bills. Or starved, because there was no way she could do both. Another state program paid for a nurse to come once a day, and check Ruby's vitals and her overall health. The nurse would stay for an hour, and that was the only real break Marie had from her home.

That was when she'd run her errands, get the shopping done, and escape. Sometimes, she'd go to the library, pick up some books, something she'd read at night, in bed, to help her get to sleep. Some days, she couldn't relax enough to fall asleep, and reading would always help her out.

"Mar-...," The loud sound interrupted her moment of peace, and Marie stood up. She smoothed her hand down her still damp jeans and took a deep breath. She knew what that sound meant. A mess had been made.

She picked up a box of gloves, the paper towels she kept off to the side for these occasions and picked up some plastic bags from the grocery store. The smell hit her as she walked down the hallway, a smell that confirmed her suspicions. She'd have to clean her mother up, wash her again, and maybe even change the bed.

She'd put fresh absorbent pads underneath her mother when she'd finished washing her, but they weren't always enough. She made one stop, in the bathroom she found a jar of mentholated ointment and swiped a couple of globs up her nose, then went into her mother's bedroom. The sadistic leer on her mother's face told her this was no accident.

Sometimes her mother was just a cruel, heartless bitch, Marie had to admit. She tried so hard to be a good girl, she thought, she tried to not be mean, to not give in to her mother's nastiness but sometimes, she hated herself for it but, sometimes she really looked forward to the day this was all over.

Marie pursed her lips and ignored the garbled cackle her mother made as she pulled the sheet down from Ruby's legs. Even the mentholated ointment couldn't keep that out of her nose, but she reminded herself not to breathe through her nose and got on with the task at hand. An hour later, just as she heard a knock at the back door, Marie was done. She'd cleaned up the worst of it, washed her mother, changed the sheets and her mother's nightdress, and had put fresh pads down.

She walked out of the room, determined not to cry. She wanted to, she wanted to so much, but she wouldn't. She remembered the way her mother had tried to use her good arm, her right arm, to push Marie's face down into the mess she'd made and felt her eyes well up. How could being born deserve so much cruelty?

She knew her mother said her father wanted her aborted, but the hateful woman never said what she'd wanted before the accident. She'd only ever said it was too late once she'd woken up and the whole world knew about her pregnancy. That no doctor would do it at that advanced state anyway. Marie suspected her mother had wanted to keep her but had changed her mind once her father died.

Marie was a bright woman, had always done well in school, and had made good grades. She was able to deduce, from what her mother had said over the years, sometimes after a few glasses of cheap wine, that her mother had become pregnant on purpose, to trap the man she'd wanted to force to marry her.

But he'd already been married to another woman, and then he'd died. Her plan, her trap, had failed.

It wasn't the kind of past people would be proud of, for

her or her mother, and her mother drank a lot when Marie was a child. She'd probably said things she didn't remember saying. Marie didn't mention those things or ask about them, for fear of her mother's anger. She'd been slapped one too many times to push her luck.

She was 26 now, and she'd spent 8 years in this miserable hell. At first, it hadn't been so bad. She'd been able to take her mother out with her, or she'd been able to go out on her own. Within a year, however, Ruby had taken to her bed and had refused to leave it. Of course, her left leg and arm wouldn't move, and the effects on her spine and hips made movement difficult, so Marie couldn't really blame her, but she'd wondered how much of her mother's problems were exaggerated.

In quiet moments, like now when she was headed into town for groceries in the old battered car that barely ran but tried, more thoughts would intrude. Her mother had always been cruel. She could be making this worse for Marie than it had to be. It was within the realm of possibility anyway.

At those times, Marie would think that maybe she could be a better daughter. But Ruby could have, also, been a much better mother.

Get Mafia's Dirty Secret Today! FREE as an ebook on major bookstores!

ALSO BY

Also by Summer Cooper

DARK DESIRES
A billionaire dark romance series
Dark Desire (FREE ebook!)
Dark Rules
Dark Secret
Dark Time
Dark Truth

BARRE TO BAR
A billionaire second chance series
Dancing With Lies (FREE ebook!)
Dancing With Temptation
Dancing With Doubt
Dancing With Guilt
Dancing With Redemption

TWISTED INTENTION
A billionaire revenge romance series

Twisted Beauty (FREE ebook!)
Twisted Love
Twisted Fate

Mafia's Obsession
A hot mafia romance series
Mafia's Dirty Secret (FREE ebook!)
Mafia's Fake Bride
Mafia's Final Play

Screaming Demons
An MC romance series full of suspense
Rough Start (FREE ebook!)
Rough Ride
Rough Choice
Rough Return
Rough Patch
Rough Road
Rough Trip
Rough Night
Rough Love
Check out Summer's entire collection at
www.summercooper.com/books

Also by Miranda Stanley

Heart Shaped Chaos
Be Mine Tonight
A Forbidden Guardian (FREE ebook!)
Escape to His Arms
You Can't Be Mine
I Still Hate You
Yours Always

Take Me Home
Tricked and Treated
Candy Cane Kisses
He's Such A D*ck
His Tokens

ABOUT THE AUTHORS

About Summer Cooper

Besides (obviously!) reading and writing, she also loves cuddling her dogs, shouting at Alexa, being upside down (aka Yoga) and driving her family cray-cray!

Follow Summer on Facebook | Instagram| Goodreads | Bookbub

Get in touch at
hello@summercooper.com

www.summercooper.com

About Miranda Stanley

Miranda is a world-traveling, genre hopping writer of contemporary and paranormal romance. A firm believer that love doesn't come in one shape, or size, or flavor, she writes people that want to break out of the roles society dictates people should have and create a new life, a new way to live, and maybe have an adventure or two along the way. She's overly fond of women who speak their minds, men who know how to listen, and spices of all varieties. After all, it would be a very boring world if every single one of us was the same, wouldn't it?

Follow Miranda on Facebook | TikTok | BookBub | Instagram

Get in touch at

https://mirandawritesbooks.wixsite.com/ mirandawritesbooks